"May I help you undress?"

Kate came forward and opened Jamie's shirt, revealing his chest, the flat bands of hard muscles, the sculpted span of his shoulders.

He started gathering up the tiny pleats of her skirt, reaching past the gauzy fabric to cup the curves of her derriere. "Jamie, wait," Kate scolded. She saw his eyes flash and chastised, "I *said* wait."

She didn't make him wait long. Only long enough for her to more or less rip his belt open and yank down his zipper with an audible *zip* of haste. The loose trousers dropped to the floor, revealing a pair of black silk boxers dotted with tiny red hearts pierced by metallic gold arrows.

Knowing she'd just lost the upper hand, she teased a little breathlessly, "Well, at least they don't say Home Of The Whopper."

Carrie Alexander has been writing for nearly five years. She was inspired to begin by reading "one of those purple-prose-and-damsels-in-distress-writing-romance-for-love-and-money articles." She lives and writes in a small town, in the Upper Peninsula of Michigan.

All Shook Up is her second book for Temptation. Her next funny, charming novel, *The Madcap Heiress,* will be published in November this year as a Harlequin Love & Laughter title. Enjoy!

Books by Carrie Alexander

HARLEQUIN TEMPTATION
536—FANCY-FREE

STOLEN MOMENTS
HIS MISTRESS

ALL SHOOK UP
Carrie Alexander

Harlequin Books

TORONTO • NEW YORK • LONDON
AMSTERDAM • PARIS • SYDNEY • HAMBURG
STOCKHOLM • ATHENS • TOKYO • MILAN
MADRID • WARSAW • BUDAPEST • AUCKLAND

ISBN 0-373-25698-1

ALL SHOOK UP

Printed in U.S.A.

Prologue

ALTHOUGH IT WAS extremely unlikely, she was sorry to say it was true. Kate Mallory had caught the bridal bouquet—definitely not by intent, and for the fourth time that year.

At age thirty-three, her previous delight in being singled out as the next potential bride had waned. The wedding guests' subsequent teasing, by now only too familiar, had begun to seem almost accusatory. *Hurry up and get married already*, Kate had imagined they were thinking. *Give someone else a chance!*

She'd done her best, this time resorting to the Skulking-at-the-Back-of-the-Crowd maneuver. But the bouquet had shot over the outstretched fingertips of the eager group—knocking off the canary yellow hat of the frantically leaping maid of honor in the process—and struck Kate smack in the chest. There'd been no graceful way to decline.

Four times, Kate thought, as her escort, a groomsman named Rodney Pfaeffle—"Rhymes with awful," he'd informed Kate with much gnashing of his horsey teeth—braked his red muscle car at her curb. Four times had to be some kind of record. One she'd never wanted to claim.

Rod revved the engine several times, eyeing Kate's lapful of stephanotis, yellow roses and crystal-beaded sprays with meaningful intent. "Heh-heh. I guess this means we're s'posed to get to know each other better?"

Kate opened her mouth, but no sound came out.

Rod twisted his broad shoulders past the steering wheel, the cascade of ruffles on his unbuttoned tuxedo shirt gaping open to reveal a dense thicket of black chest hair. His large, square face would have fit among the monoliths on Easter Island, and it was looming toward Kate even as she shrank back an equivalent distance, crushing the brim of her straw hat flat against the car window. "Gonna invite me inside?" he said, peppering the suggestion with his insinuating chuckle. "Heh-heh-heh."

She stared at his big nicotine-yellow teeth, bared again in a raffish smile. "Not this time, Rod. I'll just—" She hurriedly tumbled out of his car in a froth of crinolines, shedding petals and leaves, the long tails of her bow catching under her heels as she lurched to slam the door. "Let you go," she puffed. Her hat spun into the gutter. "Thanks for—"

Rod flipped his hand out the window in a parting gesture as his car belched a plume of noxious exhaust and screeched away from the curb. The ribbons on Kate's yellow hat spiraled in the blast of hot air.

"—the ride," she concluded, though the word that sprang to mind was *nothing.* Surely being destined to be the next bride—again—didn't have to entail Rodney Awful being the groom!

Kate gathered up her belongings and the vast folds of her ballerina-length dress and shuffled toward her gate. Boris trotted down the sidewalk, toenails clicking, a low-level growl reverberating at the back of his throat.

"Shoo," Kate said. "Go on home, Boris." Holding off the squat boxer with the toe of one of her lemon faille mules, she successfully popped through the rustic twig gate and bumped the latch down with the back of her wrist.

The dog snapped at Kate's dress through the crisscross twigs, catching the pointed tail of the bow between his teeth.

"Bad dog," Kate said, tugging. Boris clamped down with a shake of his head and a geyser of flying spit.

Disgusted, Kate yanked harder. A rumbling growl shook Boris's broad chest. He waddled two steps back, his loose jowls quivering around the length of sheer georgette.

"Boris!" Kate dropped the bouquet and the hat to pull with both hands. The fragile fabric began to tear.

"Bad dog," said a stern voice at Kate's shoulder, and Boris's jaws unlocked. He looked up with a doggy grin, his short, curled tail wiggling tentatively as Kate reeled in the gummy, bedraggled spoils. "Go home," ordered Monica Danielson, Kate's right-hand neighbor, in a voice that worked on dogs, children, husbands and telemarketers alike.

"Bore-risss," trilled Mr. Buntz, Kate's neighbor on the left side. "Silly old fellow," she heard him croon once the boxer had wormed his way back through the seven-foot hedge that surrounded his reclusive owner's yard. "Were those nasty neighbor ladies mistreating my silly old fellow again?"

Monica snorted with wordless eloquence, then picked up the bouquet and waved it about. "Oh, Kate, no. Not again!"

"Oh, Monica, yes. Again." Kate grimaced. "Take it, please. Give it to Violet with my compliments."

"That makes, what, four?" Monica said as they followed the cobbled path through an overgrown tangle of bushes and trees that crowded Kate's front yard. Golden dollops of the setting sun winked through the shrubbery.

"Four," Kate confirmed. "Four weddings, four bouquets. And it's only May!"

Monica's eyes rounded. "Can you imagine what June will bring?" It was obvious that she considered Kate's dismay over her growing bouquet collection immensely amusing.

Taking her keys from her purse, Kate swore, "As of now, I've resolved not to accept another invitation. I don't care how many June brides I know."

"But you already have," Monica reminded her. "There's Penelope's wedding the first weekend in June, and since it took her forty-seven years to get to the altar, not a soul in town is missing *that* one. And isn't your cousin Eddie's wedding coming up soon, too?"

"I'd forgotten." Kate sighed and pushed open her front door with a slumped shoulder. Apparently there was no escaping her destiny. "I'll simply have to come up with a fiancé to deflect the unwelcome attention when I catch my fifth and sixth bouquets of the year. As I inevitably will."

The only problem was there didn't seem to be a fiancé on the horizon. Determined to treat all comers fairly, Kate had met and dated plenty of possibles over the years, but none had been actual contenders. Maybe she'd try an escort service, rent a fiancé, as it were. She definitely couldn't put any of her casual dates through the ordeal of a nosy family wedding. Better still, she could hire an actor! Someone big enough and male enough for even myopic, half-deaf Great-aunt Flora to notice before she could bellow, as she had at the last Mallory wedding, "Poor Katrina! Hitting the wrong side of thirty and still a bridesmaid!"

The memory of the heads of seventy-five wedding guests swiveling Kate's way in perfect synchronization still had the power to horrify. She'd never cared for being the center of attention.

Monica was watching Kate with dark-eyed, contemplative, brow-furrowing concern, from her own comfortable seventeen-happy-years-married niche. Kate wondered why she herself hadn't been smart enough to select a husband when the pickings were fine. The obvious answer was that she'd been *too* smart for her own good; she hadn't looked up from her microscope long enough to realize that the girls who'd graduated without honors knew things that Brain-o-matic Mallory did not.

"Rod?" Monica asked, in the shorthand way they'd adopted over the years of being neighbors and friends.

Kate grimaced. "Three words—*rhymes with Pfaeffle*."

Monica's laugh percolated with its own particular zest. "Can't say as I'm surprised." Her crow's-feet crinkled. "But the question remains. Are you going out with him again?"

"He didn't ask." Kate's mood lightened at that realization. She stepped over the threshold and kicked off her shoes, thinking that at least she wouldn't have to test her devotion to equality by going out with Rodney Awful. Then again, how was she to find her destined husband if she didn't give everyone—even Rod—a whirl?

After all, catching four, count 'em, *four* bouquets had to mean something. If one believed in sentimental claptrap and groundless superstition. Which Kate usually didn't.

Then again, considering the wilting bouquet tucked under Monica's arm, she had to admit to a smidgen of stubborn hope. She plucked a yellow rose from the bunch and twirled it thoughtfully. It was purely wishful thinking, but *what if*? What if catching four out of four bridal bouquets in a matter of months actually did mean she'd soon marry...?

Dream on, her more practical side scoffed. She'd come this far without meeting Mr. Right, and catching numbers one, two and three hadn't changed her luck. Even a fourth bouquet wasn't proof. It was merely... coincidence.

What she really needed was some kind of hard data on the odds of an always-the-bridesmaid becoming a bride. Now there was an idea with some merit!

"At least the dress isn't bad," Monica observed, interrupting Kate's thought process before it reached full power.

"For a bridesmaid's dress," Kate agreed, smoothing the full skirt. It was a confection of pale yellow georgette, with a sleeveless fitted bodice. Two wide bands of sheer fabric skimmed her bare shoulders, met in a large fluffy bow anchored between her shoulder blades, then flowed all the way to her ankles. One end of the bow now terminated in a wrinkled wad of teethmarks, thanks to Boris.

"Of course, it's no iridescent aqua mermaid's sheath," Kate added with a wry chuckle, referring to the dress she'd worn to a fellow schoolteacher's early spring wedding. At that affair she'd snagged a thick bundle of dyed-to-match hyacinths despite an attempt at the It-Rebounded-Off-My-Fingertips ploy.

"Omigosh, that getup," Monica groaned, remembering the four-inch stiletto heels and jeweled headpiece. She patted Kate's shoulder. "Why don't you come on over to my yard to relax and commiserate? I've got beer. I filched it from Ed's stash before the kids chased me out of the house with their nightly bickering over loading the dishwasher."

"Maybe for a bit." A good long talk with Monica might soothe the out-of-sorts, out-of-sync feeling she'd had since catching yet another bouquet. Kate set her purse and keys on the drop-leaf table in the entryway, then shut the door behind her.

Wiggling her nylon-clad toes in the cool grass, she trusted Monica to steer her through the mysterious and not-so-mysterious lumps of the Danielson's unkept backyard. Natasha, the maker of the not-so-mysterious lumps, yipped excitedly, throwing her small furry body again and again to the limits of the chain that tethered her to the doghouse. Kate picked her way over to greet the dog with a few kindly pats. Natasha sniffed the fluttering tails of the mangled bow.

Kate sank into a folding lawn chair and accepted a beer. They drank in companionable silence, disturbed only by girlish giggles and shrieks of outrage from Monica's kitchen. At last, Kate cleared her throat to make a grave pronouncement:

"In my lifetime, I have been on 1,164 dates."

Choked with surprise, Monica abruptly lowered her beer. "No one's been on that many dates," she protested, then reflected. "Except maybe Madonna."

Since most of what Kate knew of pop culture was the result of Monica's patient explanations, she could verify only her own total. "It's true," she insisted. "I worked it out at the reception over the veal medallions in plum sauce. In my lifetime, I've been on 1,164 dates."

"Give or take."

"Well, admittedly, the number may not be as precise as I'd like. I did have to average things out to some extent. There was the dry stretch when I decided I'd had enough of college boys and would concentrate on getting my master's instead...."

"But 1,100—" Monica sputtered.

Carefully Kate balanced the beer bottle on her knee. "Monica, you married your high school sweetheart. You dipped only one toe into the primordial cesspool of the modern dating world." She closed her eyes and summoned up memories of the wildly varied representatives of the male species who'd arrived on her doorstep over the years. All of them ultimately disappointing, one way or another. "Whereas I've been submerged up to my neck for *seventeen years.*"

"True," Monica admitted grudgingly. She finished her beer, tilting her head back and sucking the last trickle down the long neck, then leaned over to set the bottle on the bumpy lawn. When she came back up she shook her curly black hair out of her eyes just the way Natasha did when Boris had sneaked past the fence. "What I don't understand is how a woman like you, a woman so thoroughly immersed in the utterly *fascinating* world of photosynthesis and chlorophyll and paramecium—" The words rolled off her tongue, proof that their backyard education sessions had been mutual. "How a woman like that manages to emerge from the lab long enough to meet, let alone date 1,164 men!"

"Technically speaking," Kate said with calm assurance, "the sum refers to dates, not men. The actual total of male acquaintances would have to be prorated according to the number of times I'd dated them. For instance, if we used a ratio of six dates to each man—"

"Let's not and say we did," Monica interrupted, knowing to what depths a conversation with Kate could sink once she began using terms like *technically speaking.* She eyed the beads of condensation accumulating on Kate's beer. "Tell me your secret instead. How do you attract so many men?"

A genuinely mystified Kate shook her head. "Secret?" She picked up the bottle, remembered she wasn't particularly fond of beer, and passed it to Monica. "There is no secret. I don't do anything."

Monica knew her friend was telling the truth, and that was the really appalling part of it. She narrowed her eyes at Kate, who was sitting erect in the webbed chair, a faraway look in her eyes, one bare, tanned arm folded so she could thoughtfully tap her index finger against the slight hollow in her chin.

That Kate was tall, long-legged, full-breasted and possessed a set of really good bones helped, of course. A lot. Monica wiggled her own curvy fanny against the tight squeeze of the lawn chair and finished Kate's beer. Nevertheless, except for being well-groomed, Kate didn't bother to take full advantage of her assets. After three years as her neighbor, Monica had finally accepted that Kate wasn't particularly aware of her looks, and truly didn't "do anything."

Kate didn't tempt, tease, flirt or seduce. She wasn't desperate, manipulative or starving for affection. If she didn't notice her own looks, neither did she seem to notice her date's. Rodney Pfaeffle had almost as good a chance at a first date with Kate as Mel Gibson. She didn't distinguish between a ten-dollars-an-hour carpenter and a three-hundred-an-hour attorney. Kate was tall, but she had no problem going out with short men. While she had the slender yet curvy figure of a beauty queen, she'd willingly dated pudgy Gary Mickles for several weeks last winter. She was super-intelligent, yet she'd found plenty to talk about with the guy who sprayed vegetables at the local grocery.

All of which explained Kate's success with men, Monica decided, mercilessly annihilating the fat mosquito that had landed on her thigh. And all of which also explained Kate's noticeable lack of success with that one *special* man. For Kate, a science teacher through and through, was aloof. She seemed to consider men just another interesting species, on a par with ferns, pond spore or *Panax quinquefolium*. After she'd studied one, noting its habitat, characteristics and mating rituals, she went on to the next with scarcely a backward glance.

It was simple, really. Kate's problem was that she'd never fallen in love.

"The problem is I've been too haphazard in my approach," Kate said suddenly. She'd stopped tapping her chin, which Monica knew meant she'd examined all sides of the problem and come to a grand conclusion. "I've relied on romance, not logic."

"Romance!" Monica repeated, stunned once again at how her brain and Kate's moved in totally opposite directions. "You have got to be kidding."

Kate didn't even hear Monica's objection; she was pre-occupied with the tiny idea that had sprung to life some minutes earlier and then blossomed into a thoroughly interesting concept. The thrill of a potential scientific quest had captured all her attention. "It's crystal clear to me now," she marveled. "I can't believe I didn't see it before tonight."

"What are you talking about?"

"The dating process. It's ridiculously outmoded." In her excitement, Kate had clenched her fingers around the brim of her bridesmaid's hat and was molding it like a milliner on fast forward. "While I've always intellectually acknowledged how far-fetched the idea of love at first sight is, I was still clinging emotionally to the notion that I'd some day meet the perfect man. Mr. Right." She made a clucking noise with her tongue. "Considering the population of this country, let alone the world, an insistence that there is one man, and one man alone, meant to be my husband is clearly romantic drivel. Bunk that should be debunked!" At that, Kate flung up her hands and the hat went sailing through the dusk like a beribboned Frisbee.

Natasha launched herself and caught it in midair, the metals links of her chain snaking through the grass with a jingle as she quickly retreated to the doghouse with her prize.

Kate didn't notice. Monica did, but didn't, at the moment, care. "I'll give you that, provisionally," she said with caution. "But I don't see how . . ."

"I've been on 1,164 dates, Monica. Odds are that lightning won't strike on the 1,165th."

"So-o-o?"

"So." Kate took a deep breath and squared her shoulders. "I'm going to forget about romance. It's too unreliable." A fanfare of trumpets sounded inside her head. "I will choose my ideal mate by computer!"

"I've got news for you, Katrina Mallory. You might have missed it when you had your nose stuck in a textbook, but someone's already thought of computer dating. And it didn't work any better than the hit-and-miss approach."

"Oh, but I don't mean dating, per se. I'm referring to the actual process of deciding which of the men I've already dated would be a suitable match. One of them, probably quite a few of them should be viable candidates for long-term monogamy."

Monica's "Uh-huh" was skeptical.

"I'll gather statistics on the men I've dated in the last year. Those that haven't married since," Kate amended. She'd once dated today's groom, before introducing him to her former college roommate, the bride. "I wonder what number would constitute a representative sampling . . . ?"

Monica just shook her head.

"So many variables go into maintaining a workable partnership. I'll have to devise equations that give the proper weight to each one." Kate began to tap her chin again. "For instance, the Career category should be subdivided into sections like Profitability, Stability, et cetera. And there will be numerous aspects to the Character and Personality categories . . ."

"What about love?" Monica interjected. "And lust?"

"Love? Lust?" Kate shrugged. "Love is illogical. Whimsical at its best. Illusory at worst. Technically speaking, what is commonly referred to as 'love' is no more than a temporary chemical reaction in the brain. The euphoria of infatuation." She cast a sidelong look at Monica. "Otherwise known as lust."

"Kate, do you think I would have stayed with Ed all these years if I didn't love him?"

"Oh, no, Monica. You misunderstand me. I believe in the existence of love. I wouldn't have undergone 1,164 dates if I didn't believe in love. And marriage. What I'm saying is that the chemical reaction lasts maybe four years and only once that cycle is over do couples find what you and Ed have—companionable, dependable, mutual affection. If they're lucky."

Monica grunted, somewhat placated. "Companionable and dependable doesn't sound all that great."

Unfazed, Kate held up one finger as if she were standing at a podium delivering a lecture. "My computer program will eliminate the vagaries of that first confusing cycle of emotion and attraction."

"But that's the fun part!"

"Yes, well." Kate cleared her throat. "In the popular vernacular of the day, I can only say—Been there, done that."

"Oh, Kate," Monica murmured with what Kate interpreted to be a sorrowful sigh, which was curious, considering that Monica was usually hugely entertained by tales of Kate's dates. Kate, too, had come to view her travails with the opposite sex with a sort of detached, tolerant amusement.

Having been awkward, homely and shy in her teen years, it was poetic justice at its most ironic that Kate had blossomed and aroused male interest only after such matters were completely unimportant to her. When the ugly duckling had finally turned into a swan, all her attention had been fixed on that darn microscope.

Although Kate hadn't quite accepted that fairy tale as her own particular truth.

Until today. Catching a fourth bridal bouquet was enough to affect anyone, even the most logical woman.

"I suppose it's true," she admitted. "My idea isn't new at all. I'd really be taking the age-old practice of matchmaking and updating it with modern technology."

Monica was exasperated. "Kate, you've never before been the slightest bit interested in rating your dates. You even rejected the standard one-to-ten scale I suggested."

Kate frowned. "And where has that policy gotten me?" She answered herself. "Thirty-three and married only to my job, that's where. Isn't it time I got serious about this husband and babies stuff?" *Before it's too late and I'm hopelessly stuck in my rut,* she added inwardly. Why, even stuffy scientists like her parents had succumbed to the biological imperative of marriage and mating.

"Ohhh, Kate." Monica moaned, *"Stuff?"* She was interrupted by the sound of water spraying against her kitchen window. From the inside. "Kids!" she barked, and Natasha squirmed out of the doghouse on her belly, Kate's well-chewed hat in her mouth.

"Are you actually serious about choosing a husband out of the *cesspool* of men you already know?" Monica got up to retrieve the hat from Natasha and missed Kate's involuntary expression of dismay.

"Maybe. Maybe not." She shifted uneasily. "These things can't be rushed. But it'll take me to the end of the summer, say, to refine the program. Which would give me plenty of time to collect a significant sampling of applicants. And since I'll be approaching thirty-four, after which the human female's fertility rate begins to decline, the timing would be ideal for me to engage in both marriage and motherhood." Kate finished triumphantly, but deep down she knew it was just easier to hide behind the dry facts of biology than admit to the truth.

She was lonely. She was tired of dating and watching from the sidelines as her friends and relatives found their mates, some of them for the second time around. However, she'd also come to see that all this falling in love malarkey was just that. Love certainly hadn't happened to her, and she'd given it 1,164 chances. If a match made by computer lacked a certain stardust and an indefinable magic, too bad. She was no longer willing to wait for love to appear out of the blue.

It was more than just Mother Nature and the four bridal bouquets driving her to do this. There was also her sense of being incomplete and out of sync. Sure, she had friends, dates, a satisfying career, her own house. But she didn't have a husband. Children.

She didn't have a family of her own. A wonderful, loving, accepting family of her own. Like Monica's.

Monica handed Kate what was left of the straw hat. "Well, good luck, sister. *Good* luck."

Kate pushed down the longing that was rising inside of her. "You sound skeptical—"

There was a crash and a wail from the kitchen. Eight-year-old Violet, Monica's youngest, burst through the screen door. "Mo-o-om!" She ricocheted back inside. "It wasn't my fault!"

"Duty calls," Monica said, walking off, muttering under her breath. At the doorstep, she turned back. "Kate, you're all wrong, you know. You have never—" A spout of water sprayed through the screen, spattering her shorts, and she turned to look into the kitchen. "What have you kids done now?" she screeched, and disappeared inside.

Kate looked at Natasha. Natasha looked at Kate's hat.

"I have," Kate said softly to the un-hat dangling from her fingertips. "I've tried it their way and it hasn't worked." Her mouth firmed as she deliberately ignored the undefined ache of longing that was probably nothing but unregenerate, thoroughly unscientific sentimentality. "Now I'm going to try it my way."

FOUR HOURS LATER, a light still burned in Kate's minuscule upstairs office under the eaves. In an atypical moment of whimsy that she gaily attributed to the late hour, her third cup of herbal tea and the pure headiness of scientific and statistical fervor, she'd decided what to call the program that was being hatched on her computer.

She named it *Love Bytes*.

1

Two months later

THE FIRST THING Kate noticed about Jamie Flynn was his quirky upper lip. She stood in the dim light of the Huckleberries foyer, half listening to the jukebox and squinting at him as her vision adjusted from the sunshine of the late July afternoon when she realized she was actually staring. She caught herself up with a little inner shake of admonition. She'd come to Mr. Flynn's bar and grill in her capacity as a schoolteacher, hoping to secure him as a chaperon for a class field trip. She definitely wasn't here as a single woman on the prowl, though she'd been feeling like one of late. After two months of catering to the voracious appetite of Love Bytes, the whole thing had become less of a thrilling scientific exercise and more of a chore. Of course, that was the number-crunching-another-dull-date part of it.

Her gaze returned unerringly to the man behind the bar. Other aspects of the project had retained their allure.

Still, Kate was determined to see Love Bytes through to its practical conclusion, preferably by the end of the summer so she could settle on her ideal mate before the new school year began. She'd decided that the wider the control group of subjects the truer the selection process, so just about every man she met was a potential prospect.

Even Mr. Flynn, the single father of one of her students.

Kate liked his quirky upper lip. Not thin, not wide, not pouty, nor hard, it was . . . curly. She imagined tracing the curves of his lip until her fingertips reached the outer corners that tilted up, not just when he smiled, but always in a way that made him look impish. And surprisingly sexy...

Katrina Mallory! Whatever are you thinking?

Kate shook herself again, to no avail. She'd have liked to say she couldn't understand what had gotten into her, but that wasn't the case. She knew all too well what was happening.

She had men on the brain. And it wasn't as uncomfortable or as cumbersome a sensation as she'd imagined it would be.

In fact, it was rather enjoyable. In a frivolous, distracting, purely I'd-sacrifice-anything-for-science sort of way, of course. She hadn't lost *all* contact with the realities of her true empirical, academic nature.

It was just that, at times, her brain had begun to take these entertaining little detours.

The man behind the bar had noticed her by now and was curious, arching his brows. Kate clasped her hands before her, fairly certain in her identification of Jamie Flynn because she'd already met him once, last March, at a parent-teacher conference. Strange how she'd missed the more intriguing aspects of his upper lip on that occasion!

"Mr. Flynn?" she asked, hesitantly approaching the massive bar. It was at least twelve feet long, a scarred, aged, highly polished curve of mellowed mahogany with a brass handrail. Kate clenched both hands on the rail as she leaned in for an even closer look—at the bartender.

"That's me," he said, giving her a cocky grin, his upper lip curling even tighter. It was a mobile lip, one that could have produced a magnificent snarl. However, Kate's new-found instincts about the male species, honed these last few months to a snappy efficiency, told her that Jamie Flynn wasn't the snarling type.

Without thinking, she leaned over the bar, her gaze dropping. Mr. Flynn was wearing pleated trousers in a rather unusual tiny black-and-white-check. He had on red suspenders, a charcoal shirt with the sleeves rolled up and a very narrow red leather tie. He wasn't overly tall, five-eleven at the most, which put him only an inch above her, but he was solid. Her eyes lingered at his midriff, that masculine trouble spot. Solid and fit, no hint of an incipient pot or poochy love handles. Visually she measured his shoulders. Muscular, too.

There was an abrupt moment of silence as the jukebox changed records, during which Kate made the clear-headed, impersonal assessment that, all in all, Jamie Flynn was a fine physical specimen, a man who'd pass on some admirable genes.

Then the jukebox clicked and Elvis Presley started singing "All Shook Up" and something strange happened inside of Kate. Suddenly there was a funny, looping sensation going on in the pit of her stomach. It felt oddly emotional, an arousal strong enough to disturb her composure if she allowed it. Masterfully, she ignored the feeling—until Mr. Flynn swiveled his hips like Elvis, reached up, loosened the knot in his tie and started unbuttoning his shirt.

Kate's hands fluttered nervously; her eyes widened. Her strictly scientific intent was history. The jukebox seemed to double its volume. *I'm all shook up.*

A couple of older guys perched on stools at the other end of the bar looked away from the muted flickering screen of a televised baseball game and snickered. A female voice shrilled from one of the shadowy booths, "Take it off, Huck!"

"What are you doing?" Kate demanded.

"Giving the customer what she wants," he said, tugging his shirt out of his trousers, unbuttoning it at the same time until she could see nearly all of his chest. That chest was muscular, appealingly smooth and sculpted, glowing a warm honey brown in the dim light. She was appalled. Entranced.

"Stop it this instant!" she insisted, gulping back a forceful desire for just the opposite.

His fingers stilled; there were two remaining buttons. "Oh, so you didn't want to examine the *menu* that closely?" he said. "I could've sworn . . ." He glanced at his other patrons apologetically. "I must be losing it, guys. Or maybe—" He smiled roguishly at Kate "—maybe the lady has already made her choice." His eyes twinkled. "Keep in mind that there are a few tasty specials not listed on the regular menu. . . ."

She gasped. Was he saying what she was afraid he was saying? Perhaps she had been a bit too obvious in her perusal of the "menu," but a true gentleman wouldn't have called her on it! The loopy feeling in her stomach radiated ripples of mortification, turning her face a lively shade of pink. Luckily she was saved from having to respond by the older woman who'd left her booth to hang on to the rail beside Kate.

"Aw, Huck," she said, lazily draping her scrawny torso over the bar. "Don't stop jes' when it's gettin' entertainin'."

He shrugged and started rebuttoning. "Sorry, Millie. The health inspector could walk in and catch me bare-chested."

"Might be *she's* the health inspector," suggested one of the guys with a nod at Kate.

"Come to do some inspecting!" his fellow barfly chortled.

"Hmm." The bartender turned his attention back to her. "And what do you say?"

Guiltily, Kate jerked her gaze away from Mr. Flynn's chest and up to his open, friendly face. "No, I'm not the health inspector," she snapped, reluctant now to admit to her true identity after such an ignominious beginning. She swallowed her pride. "My name is Kate Mallory, Mr. Flynn. I'm your daughter Suzannah's natural science teacher."

"A schoolteacher," Millie said, lurching backwards and plopping onto a stool as she examined Kate. "Don't see much of them in here, hey, Huck?"

Flynn peered over the bar in a perfect imitation of Kate, his gaze lingering first on her lips—which warmed precipitously—then dropping to her feet before rising in a leisurely, thorough once-over. "Nope. Sure don't see much of 'em."

Kate's flush deepened. "Mr. Flynn, I—"

He spoke at the same moment. "Why don't you take that—" he flipped his hand up and down, indicating the loose, shawl-collared coat she wore "—*parka* off, teach? You look kinda warm."

Ignoring any innuendo, Kate decided that she was in fact warm and slipped off the lightweight cover-up to reveal the sleeveless dove gray sheath beneath. She folded the matching jacket neatly and draped it over the handrail, then sat down beside Millie, who had been watching their byplay beneath droopy eyelids.

"Much better," Jamie Flynn said with obvious masculine appreciation. "What'll you have, teach?"

Kate studied the eight inches of bare chest he was still showing, noting that the strip of red leather had worked itself free from his collar to rest between his nicely defined pectorals like a lick of fire.

"Something to drink?" he prompted, his amused tone making her blink. She returned her attention to his intriguing upper lip. She saw laughter there.

Her mouth as arid as the Sahara, she said, "Um, I guess I could have a, ah—"

"Do her, Huck," called a natty chap who'd just entered. Kate looked around and saw that in the ten minutes since she'd arrived, the sleepy bar and grill was beginning to exhibit signs of life. It was still a little early for happy hour, but most of the accumulating patrons didn't look like nine-to-five types anyway.

"Go on. Do her," someone else said. "Yeah, do her, do her," several others chimed in.

Do her? Alarmed, Kate braced her heels against the rungs of the stool and spun back to face Jamie Flynn, her spine rigid.

He placed both hands on the bar and stared into her eyes for a very long moment. "White wine spritzer," he finally announced to the room, then shrugged, hands up, as the onlookers groaned in unison. "Afraid that's all I see, folks."

Kate watched suspiciously as he filled a glass partway with white wine, squirted it with a blast of fizzy seltzer and slid the glass toward her on a red cocktail napkin.

"White wine spritzer," scoffed Millie. She shook her head dismissively and flipped a long braid of iron gray hair over her right shoulder. With a practiced expertise, she whirled her stool around and engaged the British-accented newcomer in a cozy conversation.

Kate took a sip of the drink she might have ordered if she'd have had the chance. "What was all that about, Mr. Flynn?"

"Most folks call me Jamie. Or Huck," he said. He'd rebuttoned his shirt and was pulling its collar back inside the loosened red tie. "Teach."

Kate made a face. 'Teach' wasn't bad, as nicknames went. Somewhat unimaginative, but not, thank heaven, 'Big Red' or 'Strawberry.'

Her students called her Ms. Marshmallow, although she wasn't supposed to know that. Sometimes they even called

her Fungus-head. "What was all that about . . . Jamie?" she
tried again, tentative about the name although it seemed to
suit him. She wasn't committing to "Huck."

He drew a beer from the tap and set it in front of Millie's
friend. "Just a little amusement for the regulars." He collected a twenty at the far side of the bar and returned to
Kate's end to make change on a tall, gilded cash register, so
old-fashioned it actually went *ka-ching* when he pressed the
right button.

Licking foam off her upper lip, Millie swiveled back toward Kate. "Huck's a talented guy. Always was. Grew up
in joints like this, learnt his trade early, am I right, m'boy?"

"That's right," Jamie said shortly as he glided past them.
He was back a second later, leaning against a chrome espresso machine, arms folded, flashing Kate his killer grin.

"What is this talent, exactly?" she asked Millie, watching Jamie out of the corner of her eye and liking what she
saw, in spite of herself. Although he was physically a fine
specimen, she already suspected he'd score well below acceptable in other Love Bytes categories. He might deserve
an entry, but he'd never be a contender.

Millie was sneaking another sip of the dapper Brit's beer,
as he coaxed "Tell her, ducks."

She smacked her lips, her head weaving slightly. "S'like
this, teach—"

Jamie came forward and pushed a bowl of doughy
homemade pretzels toward Millie, thereby nudging the mug
out of her reach. He turned to Kate. "It's like this, teach,"
he murmured, cupping her chin in the palm of his hand and
tilting her face up toward his. "I look deep into a new customer's eyes—" His voice was low and somehow intimate
despite the escalating bar sounds in the background.

So far, Kate had been concentrating on Jamie's mouth and
chest; she hadn't fully taken note of the pleasant hand-

someness of his even features. He had a strong, straight nose and fine-grained skin that was as sunburnished and bursting with health as a homegrown peach. He had a square jaw, wide cheekbones, noble forehead. And red hair.

She had reason to despise red hair.

"...divine their innermost secrets..." he was saying.

Regardless of the red hair, Kate had to struggle to suppress a deliciously telling shiver, not altogether successfully. The feel of Jamie's palm under her chin was provoking impulses that were disconcerting to a woman as levelheaded as herself. She felt a warmth, a tingling, a physical yearning to roll her head against his hand and purr like a kitten. When her eyelids started to lower indolently, she forced them back up and returned her gaze to his hair.

Not even that worked, because by this time his hair wasn't looking so bad. It wasn't a bright, carroty red or a pinkish-yellowish-strawlike clump. It was a velvety auburn, quite thick and wavy on top, trimmed on the sides but just overgrown enough to curl around his upturned collar and tickle his ears. It would probably feel like rich silk slipping through her—a woman's fingers.

Jamie was still whispering. "...define their wildest dreams..."

Seeing as how not even *she* had defined her wildest dreams, she certainly hoped he didn't have that power.

At Kate's expression of horror, Jamie's wide hazel eyes seemed to laugh, the slivered shards of emerald in his irises glinting with the mischief she'd already discerned in his quirky upper lip. "And distill that knowledge into the drink that speaks to the customer's very soul." With a flourish, he finished, letting the tip of his thumb just barely skim her lower lip before removing his hand altogether.

Kate slammed shut her gaping mouth with an audible click of her teeth, then gulped like a fiend at the drink he'd chosen for her.

"I'm a gin fizz with a twist," Millie boasted. "The next morning, I'm a Red Snapper."

"Glenlivet Scotch for me," said her British neighbor, tugging on his limp ascot. "Quite rightly."

"And I'm a white wine spritzer?" Kate croaked. "That's the distillation of my...soul?"

"What can I say?" Jamie responded with a blameless shrug. "It's a gift." He ambled off to attend to his other customers, swaggering, cocksure and, Kate suddenly decided, tremendously annoying.

She was not a white wine spritzer!

Was she?

As even more customers arrived, Jamie was joined by another bartender. He was a short swarthy type named El Gato, although Kate couldn't be certain because of the growing cacophony at Huckleberries. She watched the pair work the bar and booths with a seamless, bantering ease, and began recalling the details of her first and only other meeting with Mr. Jamie "Huck" Flynn.

Theirs had been a morning appointment, and Jamie had arrived ten minutes late for his fifteen-minute slot. He'd slouched in a student desk, wearing frayed jeans and a cut-off sweatshirt, looking not much older than a teenager himself. A very dissolute teenager, she remembered thinking at the time. There'd been stubble on his jaw and he'd smelled of booze and cigarettes. After he'd only half listened, bleary-eyed, to her spiel about his daughter Suzannah's lackadaisical work habits and unfulfilled potential, she'd labeled him as an uncooperative parent.

But then his daughter had shown up at the summer school science class that Kate had suggested. Surprisingly enough,

Suzannah had been mostly faithful in her attendance and improved her attitude along with her grades.

Kate sipped her drink and mulled over what that could mean. She was willing to admit that her first impression of Jamie Flynn might have been mistaken. Perhaps working a late shift at Huckleberries had accounted for his rather ripe appearance at their meeting. Owning a bar wasn't a dishonorable career, after all, though Kate took a dim view of those who served alcoholic beverages to minors, and certainly anyone associated with putting drunk drivers on the road.

Not that she had any evidence against Jamie Flynn in that regard. Then again, Millie was looking like she might be a bit snookered, or was *snockered* the correct slang for her state of inebriation? Despite Monica's best efforts, Kate was never quite caught up on the current vernacular.

She admired, even envied Jamie's easy rapport with his customers. He joshed, charmed, consoled and back-slapped. When a raucous dispute about the Milwaukee Brewers' lone World Series appearance broke out between two guys parked at the end of the bar, Jamie matter-of-factly reeled off the correct statistics and averted further rancor with another round of pretzels and beer. Kate decided that handling a bar full of colorful characters was not unlike controlling a classroom of hyper thirteen- and fourteen-year-olds.

So she sat and sipped and watched Jamie Flynn work, ostensibly because she was waiting for a chance to speak to him about his daughter. She absorbed the slightly shabby but warm and friendly ambience of Huckleberries. She plugged a quarter into the jukebox and played "All Shook Up," hoping no one would notice it was the second time she'd done it. And she found herself staying long past the time she would have normally given up and gone home to check on the progress of her butterfly cocoons and experimental seedlings.

BY THE TIME it was officially happy hour, Jamie had grown accustomed to the feel of the schoolteacher's gaze following him around the bar. He'd even come to like it.

When Kate Mallory had walked into Huckleberries, all covered up and tightly wound, openly dissecting him as if he were a dead frog in a biology lab, he'd been reminded of the failings of his own school days. He'd been the disreputable class goof-off. Knowing that Ms. Mallory would most likely give him a failing grade, he'd used humor, as usual, to protect himself. Who'd have suspected that his impromptu, playful striptease would spark an improbable attraction between them?

But it had. Even for a guy who'd flunked high school chemistry, there was no mistaking that what was happening between him and the teach was pure sexual chemistry.

Happy hour segued into the dinner rush, meaning that the waitresses and cooks bore the brunt of the workload and Jamie could take a breather. He went into the kitchen to check out the remains of Whistler's picked-over hors d'oeuvre buffet.

"Is that Kate Mallory, of all people, still sitting at the bar?" Whistler asked, nodding toward the service window between the bar and the kitchen. He continued chopping parsley without looking down, his fingers and the blurred knife flecked with tiny green bits.

Jamie sent up a prayer to his insurance agent. "Do you know her?" he asked, loath as he was to distract the knife-wielding Whistler.

"Sure. She teaches school with Charity." Whistler paused to wave his knife expressively, then started in on a zucchini, still without looking. A neat row of slices appeared on the butcher block. Whistler, a fifty-four-year-old refugee of the sixties, retained all ten fingertips. "Her field's biology, I believe."

"What does Charity say about her?" A flower child turned earth mother, Charity Castle had been Whistler's live-in lover for the past thirty-odd years. She taught English and creative writing at Suze's junior high and didn't believe in making excuses or buckling under to convention. Nor did she believe in evaluating, grading and labeling students as if they were cans of corn. She and Whistler were Suze's grandparents and Jamie's next best thing to blood family. There were even times he wished they could have been the *only* parents he'd known, but that was a guilty wish he rarely allowed himself. He didn't believe in making namby-pamby excuses any more than Charity did.

Whistler ate a wedge of cucumber off the tip of his lethal knife. "Vichyssoise," he said contemplatively.

"I don't see cold soup going over with this crowd."

Whistler grunted in agreement. "According to Charity, Kate Mallory is vichyssoise," he explained. "A cold dish that puts slobs off, but yields up depths of enjoyable taste to the discerning palate."

The idea of the cool Ms. Mallory being an acquired taste appealed to Jamie, although nobody had ever accused him of coveting a Michelin star, or even a good review by the local weekly's movie-theater-restaurant critic. "Were those Charity's exact words?"

"Naw," Whistler confessed. "Char's exact words were probably more along the line of 'Live and let live.'"

"So, you don't actually know anything about her?"

Whistler flicked the point of the knife upward. "I got eyes."

Jamie bypassed the cold deep-fried zucchini sticks and selected a plateful of well-browned mini bacon-quiche tarts. "Which means?"

"Let's just say she appears to be ripe for the plucking . . ." Whistler nudged him. "If a joker like you's up to the job."

Jamie took the plate and returned the nudge. "I can pluck with the best of 'em, not that it's any of your business." He backed through the swinging door. "Watch and learn, hippie man. Maybe you'll pick up a few pointers and get Charity to the altar."

"Who says I want her there?" Whistler roared after him.

Jamie offered the tartlets to Roger and Rex, both of whom were too stubborn to give up their usual stools at the end of the bar even though they were feuding. He moved on to Millie and Cecil Apthorpe, the frayed but genteel pseudo-British expatriate who occasionally lapsed into a Midwest twang when he forgot to put on his accent. Finally he offered a tiny quiche to Kate and took the last for himself. "Whistler says hi."

"Whistler?" Kate asked, midnibble.

Jamie nodded toward the kitchen, where the balding Whistler was wildly brandishing his knife as he issued orders to the assistant fry cook. "Like Cher and Roseanne, my chef goes by only one name."

"Oh, I know him. He's Charity Castle's husb—um, her—"

"Lifemate," Jamie supplied. "Also Suze's grandfather."

"Suze?" Kate repeated, again midnibble.

"You do remember my daughter? The reason, besides white wine spritzers, you came to Huckleberries?"

"Of course. Suzannah." Visibly flustered, Kate swallowed and wiped her hands on a napkin, then lifted them to her straight, shoulder-length brown hair, smoothing it and tucking it behind her ears. "Suzannah, your daughter," she mumbled to herself, eyes averted. "My student."

Jamie chuckled softly. Beneath long pale lashes, Kate's green eyes were shining, her cheeks were flushed a rosy red. There was an intriguing ripeness about her lips—one that hadn't been there when she'd entered Huckleberries all prim and proper and schoolmarmish. Jamie found himself wondering about their taste and texture. Sweet and virginal? Warm and soft and pliable? Or spiced with an undercut of hidden sensuality?

When she forgot to firm it up, Kate's lower lip looked as ripe and succulent as the grapes Whistler grew for his homemade wine. What would it be like to kiss a schoolteacher? How would it feel to have Kate Mallory's lips fitted to his?

"I spoke with Suzannah after class this morning," Kate said, having pulled herself together. "Today was the deadline to return the signed permission slips for the overnight field trip I'd planned for the summer school science students. We're going to the Crooked River Wildlife Sanctuary and the adjoining state campground."

"Quite a mouthful," Jamie said noncommittally.

"Suzannah didn't turn in her form." Lips firmed, Kate rested her arm along the handrail and leaned forward. "And I guess you *forgot* to read the letter about how I needed some parents to volunteer as chaperons."

"Guess I did . . ." Jamie had little doubt that Kate would be shocked if she knew how her breasts appeared to him, plumped by her forearm, delectably mounded beneath the round-necked bodice of her prissy little gray dress. Nor did she seem to realize that her doubled rope of garnet and silver beads was looped around her right breast in such a way that a guy couldn't help but imagine slipping his tongue along the same path, and raining tiny hot kisses down into the shadowed depths of her cleavage . . .

"I need a man," she said emphatically, playing right into Jamie's erotic fantasy.

He looked unswervingly into her eyes until she blinked in consternation. "To fill—" she cleared her throat "—to be the last chaperon. I've managed to convince Monica Danielson, Kirsten's mother. And Gordon Hodge, Gregory Gordon's father, is donating his time. Plus myself, that makes three chaperons for sixteen kids. If we had another man . . . ?" Her eyebrows arched hopefully.

Instantly Jamie backed off, raising his hands to deflect her plea. "Don't look at me, teach. I've got a business to run."

She glanced around, pointedly taking note of the busy waitresses, cooks and Manny Delgado, the other bartender. "Two days," she said. "One night. Not a lot to sacrifice for the education of your daughter."

"Suze probably doesn't even plan to go."

Kate frowned. "She says she does."

"First I've heard of it."

"I would imagine there are quite a few things about your daughter that you don't know. Things more important than labeling people's souls as cocktails."

Jamie narrowed his eyes at her unnecessarily snippy tone. "What's that supposed to mean?"

"Nothing," she said, immediately backing off. "Forget it." She flipped open her envelope purse. "What do I owe you?"

"It's on the house, teach," he drawled. The name was spoken as a subtle taunt this time. She poked a five across the bar and he shoved it back into her hand. Her pouting lower lip was making him feel guilty about refusing to be a chaperon, and he felt guiltier yet for being an unconventional parent. He'd thought he'd come to grips with that.

"Look, Ms. Mallory, I'm just not into these kind of things, okay?"

"What kind of things?" Her tone tried for schoolmarm, but her lips betrayed pure wounded female.

"These organized, by-the-book outing kind of things. I'd make a lousy chaperon."

She looked him up and down, not meanly or icily, but not in her previous woman-to-man way, either. "You're probably right," she conceded, and suddenly he wasn't pleased that she'd agreed so easily. "I must have been suffering from a moment of temporary desperation."

Gee, thanks. "Sorry."

"Oh, don't worry yourself. I've got no end of candidates." Waving an airy goodbye, Kate slid off the barstool and made her way toward the door. Jamie was left with the curious suspicion that they hadn't been on the same wavelength. But was that any wonder?

He heaved a huge sigh. It was probably just as well things hadn't worked out. Kate Mallory wasn't his type. Never had been. Never would be. Definitely not. No way. "Damn fine legs though," he muttered as she pushed through the foyer door without a backward look.

Manny, on his way to the cash register, heard him and cupped his hands at his chest. "And lotsa-lotsa in the balcony."

Jamie tapped his temple. "Even more up here. Who needs the aggravation?"

Manny slammed the cash drawer and struck an orator's pose that drew the attention of the regulars. "And the mighty Jamie has struck out," he intoned theatrically into a momentary hush, putting the appropriate coda to the whole affair.

To the catcalls of his ungrateful patrons, Jamie exited, bar left.

KATE'S FINGERS PAUSED above the keyboard. Would it be too terribly subjective if she entered the word *yummy*? Absolutely. Could she get away with *sinfully sexy*? Unequivocally no. So far, what she had was:

Subject: #34JF
  Status: Widower, approximate age 35
  Dependents: One daughter, Suzannah, age 14
  Occupation: Owner of bar/restaurant
  Education: Unknown*
  Physical description:

She was supposed to stick to the basics at this point: height, weight, hair and eye color, outstanding characteristics. Only the in-depth evaluation phase got into the varying degrees of Sexual Attraction and Physical Response, male/female.

Now Kate was wondering if she'd given those considerations enough weight in the overall scheme of things. When she'd written the Love Bytes program she'd included them because of their initial importance, but downgraded their effect on each subject's ultimate score so as to keep the proper perspective. Surely Compatibility and Character were more important categories in the long run.

Of course they were. Her brain knew it, her gut knew it, possibly even her heart knew it. Absently Kate rubbed her palm over her thigh. It was the less obedient parts of her anatomy that were giving her grief.

And what was she doing anyway, opening up a file on Jamie Flynn—a mere acquaintance, not even a date—when she had a folder of notes on the extremely viable Professor Cotter Coleman to collate? With a cluck of impatience, Kate hit the delete key and watched subject #34JF disappear from the computer screen. "Forget it," she muttered.

If only it could be so easy to delete him from her imagination.

Resolutely Kate buckled down and she'd made it halfway through Cotter's impressive but not exactly pulse-escalating update when the dingdong of the doorbell echoed through the silent house. Her gaze flew to the clock even as she saved the information on Cotter and exited Love Bytes. Who'd be crazy enough to come visiting at five minutes to midnight?

She ducked into her bedroom and pulled a pair of sweatpants up under the baggy T-shirt she'd intended to sleep in, then stepped into the neon orange flip-flops she usually limited to the beach and Monica's backyard. Not a pretty picture, but unannounced visitors deserved no better.

The rubber thongs slapped against her bare feet as she made her way downstairs. "Who is it?" she asked cautiously at the front door. A man-shaped shadow shifted behind the frosted-glass inset.

"Jamie Flynn."

Kate swayed. She actually had to put her hand out to catch her balance. "Do you realize how late it is?" she rasped, her pulse zooming up the Physical Response-Female scale so quickly it was in danger of going off the chart altogether.

"Hey, teach, time's a relative thing. Huckleberries is still kicking."

"I'm sure," she murmured, tilting her forehead against the glass.

"Don't put yourself out, teach. It's not like I expect you to open up, or anything."

Kate licked her lips. She couldn't help but apply another meaning to his words, one that had the potential to upset her equilibrium even more. What was it about Jamie Flynn that kept her so off balance, so shook up?

"I'll just slip this under the door," he said to placate her. "And then I'm outta here."

Kate looked down as a single half sheet of photocopied paper appeared at her feet. Even before she picked it up, she recognized the field trip permission slip. Jamie's signature was as she would have expected: big, bold, scrawled beyond the designated line with a slapdash flourish. The paper was crinkled and there was a dried stain of spattered spillage on the other side. She smiled.

Suddenly afraid that he *had* left, she threw open the door. Jamie stood on the doorstep, smiling a Cheshire cat smile at her from beneath his shaggy auburn forelock.

"You needn't have done this," Kate told him with a halfway-to-bashful shrug. "Suzannah could have brought the slip in tomorrow."

"You said today was the deadline."

In the living room, a mantel clock began to chime the hour and Jamie's broad smile shifted into a boyishly charming grin. "Guess I just made it." His eyes looked like chips of polished brown agate striped with green, copper, gold. Kate's pulse thudded heavily in response and she decided she should get her blood pressure checked. Or maybe just stay out of moonlight at the witching hour.

"I'm not really that strict." She hesitated. "But thanks."

"Did you find your man?" His own slight hesitation seemed intentional. "Your chaperon?"

Was everything he said a double entendre, or was it just her? "Not yet," she admitted reluctantly. She would never reveal that although she'd tapped into school files on her computer fully intending to consult the roster of her students' parent's phone numbers, she'd ended up rereading Suzannah Flynn's records instead. And coming within a keystroke of making her father a Love Bytes candidate.

"So I can still volunteer?"

Kate swayed again. "I thought—"

"So did I. Second thoughts."

"You really want to do it?" *Oh, Kate, now everything you say has another meaning!*

"I'll give it a try."

Too late, Kate realized that having Jamie along on an overnight field trip might not be a smart move. Not when it was just as likely the chaperons would need chaperons themselves . . . if she got lucky.

"I'm thinking it might be an experience I shouldn't miss," Jamie said. He'd edged closer to the opened door and now put his hands on either side of the jamb, cocking his head and measuring the startled whites of Kate's eyes. The timbre of his lowered voice was soothing and seductive. "All that communing with nature. Romping through the wildflowers, rolling in clover, sleeping under the stars . . ."

"With sixteen raging adolescents," she reminded him.

He laughed. "Any chance we could leave them home?"

She shook her head, smiling foolishly.

"I've got to get back to the bar," Jamie finally said; it was either that or give into temptation and kiss her. Of course he'd have preferred the latter, especially since Kate was looking all cuddly and touchable in her frumpy clothes; her face was unguarded and expressive. He steeled himself with the knowledge that there would be another chance, unless he changed his mind between now and then, which was always possible.

He wasn't exactly sure why he'd come, but he hadn't been able to resist. A lack of willpower was a family inheritance, he'd reasoned on the way over, not just a namby-pamby excuse for indulging his overwhelming but probably doomed attraction to Kate Mallory.

"Can I ask you a question?" she said softly when he was about to leave. The nervous wiggle of her bare toes was enticing. "Why did you describe me as a white wine spritzer?"

He smiled. For some reason, that had really gotten under her skin. "It's a conventional choice," he explained. "A drink for people who really don't like to drink, or don't drink often."

"Oh." Kate's features puckered. "Is that all?"

"It's also . . ." Weakening, he let one palm skate along her bare arm, and swallowed hard as he savored this first small caress of her lightly tanned skin. Then he skimmed his hand down the thin shirt that was bunched half in, half out of the waistband of her sweatpants. His fingertips grazed her thigh. "It's also a drink for women who worry about keeping their figure. Needlessly, in cases of schoolteachers with the sleek lines and racy curves of a million-dollar Thoroughbred."

Kate was speechless.

"Besides, I could hardly reveal in public what I'd actually discovered after looking deep into this particular schoolteacher's eyes." Eyes that were glistening like a forest pond in the moonlight. Eyes that made him want to dive in and linger long after the moon had gone down.

Kate made a questioning sound deep in her throat.

"Which was that, despite what your white-wine-spritzer surface says—" he put his whispering lips near her ear, so close they touched the silk of her loose hair "—you and I know that somewhere deep down inside Ms. Kate Mallory is a strawberry margarita woman."

Kate's head jerked back, her cheeks instantly aflame. "You can't know that! How could you know that?"

But Jamie was already strolling away through her tangled, out-of-control garden, his knowing chuckle carrying on the warm summer air. He lifted his hands, his shoulders shifting in a repeat of his blameless shrug. "What can I say, Kate? It's a gift."

2

MONICA TURNED and rested her chin on the back of the seat. "What are you thinking about, Kate?"

Cocktails, Kate thought. Margaritas, specifically, but more importantly, not just your standard, run-of-the-mill margaritas. Oh, no, she was thinking—always and for-ever—about *strawberry* margaritas . . .

Kate looked back over her shoulder at Jamie Flynn, who was stretched out sideways on one of the bench seats in the middle of the school bus. He was wearing sunglasses, a pansy-purple tank top, long baggy cotton shorts in a black, lavender and hot pink zebra stripe pattern and high-topped sneakers with neon laces. His propped-up legs and the bare arms crossed behind his head were brown and firm and muscular—disturbingly sturdy in a manly way that said, "Here I am and there's no way you can avoid me." With the July sunshine glancing off his tousled auburn hair, he was, to say the least, a vivid presence. This wasn't the first time she'd covertly examined him since they'd departed the school parking lot an hour earlier.

But this was the first time he'd caught her at it.

Her first clue was his slanted, cocky grin. Before she could react, he'd uncrossed one arm, snicked his sunglasses down an inch, winked, tapped the dark glasses in place again and settled back to resume his nap. She whipped her head around, clenching both fists on the brim of her pith helmet and attempted to tug it all the way down to her cringing shoulders.

Monica gurgled. "I guess that's answer enough." Her dancing eyes took their own masculine pulchritude inventory. "Not that I can blame you."

"Oh, *please*," Kate muttered. "Jamie Flynn is not my type."

"Thoughtcha didn't have a type," Monica singsonged.

Kate frowned. Out of a sense of fair play and because of her strong memories of being the one never chosen, she'd always tried not to acknowledge a preference for one type of man. "Well, Love Bytes does," she said, risking another quick glance at Jamie from beneath her brim. "And he is not it."

"Why don't you let your computer decide that," Monica suggested. She brushed back the corkscrew wisps of hair that were already escaping her topknot and tried to look as scholarly as Kate. "Purely in the interests of a scientific objectivity, of course."

Even though the busload of gossipy students were making way too much noise to overhear their chaperons' conversation, Kate leaned forward to hiss into Monica's ear. "Are you saying that I should date Jamie Flynn?" It was hard to sound outraged and still keep her voice barely above a whisper.

"Why not? You've given every other single man you've met a shot at catching the Love Bytes golden ring. I don't see any reason why such an interesting prospect as Jamie should be excluded from going for the glory."

Because she had no good answer—nor an excuse—Kate sat back and fumed. Monica considered the ideal husband computer program nothing but a hugely uproarious joke. Historically speaking, the inventive ideas of great minds had usually suffered public scorn at their outset. Look at Christopher Columbus and the flat earth advocates.

Kate bit her lip and sneaked another peek at Jamie. If only she didn't feel quite so much as if she were hovering at the brink of a vast, unknown and extremely dangerous abyss herself!

The bus jounced and rattled as the driver turned it onto a blacktop two-lane road as ridged as a washboard. Kate recognized the dense evergreen forests of the Wisconsin state parkland that bordered the wildlife sanctuary. She'd taken many groups of science students here over the years to give them the chance to explore nature firsthand. Of course the kids spent more time goofing off than they did concentrating on their fieldwork, but they had studied diligently all summer and deserved some fun.

And what of herself? She'd worked hard all year. Didn't she deserve a bit of fun, too?

Forcibly keeping herself from checking out what Jamie was doing now, Kate instead looked to the front seat, where Gregory Gordon Hodge, a straight-A student whose complicated science project she'd been supervising over the summer, sat with his father. Gordon Hodge was a successful engineer, divorced, and mildly good-looking if you liked brainy square peg types, which Kate thought she should.

Gordon was also reliable, responsible, respectable— everything that Jamie apparently was not. He would score high on the Love Bytes rating scale. Jamie would not . . . except perhaps when it came to the intensity of the chemical reaction of the frivolous "infatuation" period, which only lasted a measly four years anyway. Four years was a piffle. Infatuation was fleeting. Chemistry was fine in the laboratory, but ultimately useless in her quest for the ideal husband.

And strawberry margaritas would probably give her a hangover.

So much for "Huck" Flynn, Kate resolved. There was more than one Love Bytes candidate on this bus. And Gordon Hodge looked as if he'd recognize a quality Chardonnay when he saw one!

"YOU CAN BE amateur naturalists for the rest of your lives," Kate said to the students gathered around her. "Open your eyes, train your senses. Keep in touch with the fascinating world that lives not only here at the sanctuary but all around you—under your feet and over your head, even in your backyard. Explore, appreciate, identify, question! Never lose what Rachel Carson called the 'sense of wonder' and you will be a rich person no matter what your future profession."

Jamie watched with admiration. Kate's face was luminous as she swung her arms in graceful arcs, indicating the clear azure sky above, the shadowed forest before them and behind the lowland marshes where they'd just completed a bog walk. Her unrestrained enthusiasm had transferred itself to even the most uninspired of the summer school students.

Suze, he was glad to note, had been on her best behavior. Much as he hated playing the heavy, he'd threatened her with the potential confiscation of her most treasured possession—her hot-pink-and-clear-Lucite telephone—to ensure it. For some strange reason, it had seemed important to elevate his parental standing in Kate Mallory's eyes.

And dichotomous green eyes they were. They could be cool or intense, aloof or rapt, guarded, then just as quickly warmly inviting—all beneath the brim of her ridiculous pith helmet.

Although Jamie was considered a ladies' man by his buddies at Huckleberries, in the past few hours he'd come to see even more clearly that Kate was the type of woman he'd always considered out of his league. She was classy without trying, subtly but essentially beautiful; she was caring, generous and smart as a whip to boot. She'd grown up with expectations as high as his had been low. Kate was all-star material, whereas he'd spent his life in the minors. Maybe he'd felt stifled there sometimes, but at least he'd finally found home base.

Yet, even with all the rationalizing in the world, there was still something about Kate he couldn't help wanting.

He wanted to know her.

He wanted to impress her.

Damn, he just *wanted*. He wanted Kate Mallory to look at him and like him, and want him—maybe even love him. And he wanted something else from her, something deep and important that he couldn't even define.

For a man who took each day as it came, such a realization was like suddenly eyeballing the worm in the tequila. It was sobering as hell.

KATE HAD DIVIDED the students into four groups. After short lectures, she sent one group off with the fussbudgety Gordon Hodge to study tree bark and another with the unsqueamish Monica Danielson to gather insects. She assigned Jamie's quartet the task of identifying wildflowers, aiming them toward a clearing of burnt-over deadwood that she pointed out was rife with fuchsia fireweed.

Jamie sidled over to her and stood two inches closer than her personal space allowed. "If you think I know my spleenworts from my lady's slippers, you've got another thing coming, teach."

Kate flinched, but she didn't step away. A good sign. "You can read, can't you?" She held up one of the field guides she'd supplied to the students.

"If I concentrate real hard."

"And you can look at the pictures." When she began flipping pages, he plucked the book out of her hands.

"What's this? A riddle." He held the guide open at a photo of a rose-purple thistle. "What's prickly and spiny, but the color of a strawberry margarita on top?"

Reflexively Kate patted the crown of her hat. "Please return my—"

"Bull thistle," Jamie said, avoiding her snatching hands, "or Kate Mallory?" He turned to the detailed description in the back pages. "Hmm. Handle only with kid gloves."

"That's no riddle, that's *Cirsium vulgare*," Kate said brusquely, retrieving her book. "And I'll thank you to catch up to your group before they start uprooting endangered species." Armed with a backpack of butterfly nets, she stomped off toward her own group. She cut quite a figure in her pith helmet, camouflage camp shirt and the sturdy safari pants she'd tucked into wool socks pulled above her hiking boots.

Jamie bided his time. Eventually with some subtle maneuvering he managed to meet up with Kate's group at the edge of a clearing that sloped down to the trickling Crooked River. Butterflies danced in the sunlight; Queen Anne's lace and buttercups foamed white and yellow beside a hazy sea of blue.

Ostentatiously Jamie pointed to the blue flowers as he walked over to where Kate was kneeling in the grass helping a student identify a butterfly. "Forget-me-not," he said.

Kate looked up as the student returned to the group. "I couldn't if I tried."

Grinning, he halted directly before her in a widespread stance, his hands tucked into the pockets of his zebra-stripe shorts. "Finally the frosty Ms. Mallory begins to melt."

Kate rolled her eyes. "Don't use that lady-killer grin on me, Huckleberry Flynn." She reached into one of the flapped pockets that paraded up either side of her pant legs.

She'd been pulling useful items out of them all day: tweezers, a pocket microscope, things she'd called an insect aspirator and a larva tin, string, butterfly envelopes, and a killing bottle filled with deadly cotton balls, the demonstration of which had made the female students recoil and the male ones bluster.

This time Kate withdrew a slim can of bug dope. Without asking, she shook it and sprayed Jamie's legs. He watched, bemused, as she took off her hat, lifted the magnifying glass that hung on a leather thong around her neck and began to examine his calf, up close and personal.

"You didn't read the handout about Lyme disease, did you? The one I sent home with all the students?" Her tone was disappointingly clinical.

"I meant to . . ."

She coughed. "Uh, yes, well, if you had, you would've known enough not to wear shorts." Her nose brushed his kneecap as she plucked something off the inside of his leg with the handy tweezers. She held it up for him to see, the magnifying glass enlarging her iris to the size of a two-hundred-dred karat Colombian emerald. "Don't worry, it's just a wood tick," she said. "The smaller deer ticks are the ones that carry the Lyme disease spirochete."

"Really, Kate, you do possess one silver tongue," Jamie teased. "Why, I bet you could charm a bear out of a honey tree with talk like that."

Kate ducked her chin to hide her grin; sunshine gilded her hatless head. Jamie was surprised by the distinctly reddish apricot glow to what he'd thought was her bland medium-brown hair. He sat beside her in the grass and looked closer. Nope, must've been a trick of the light. Her hair was just plain brunette.

"For a second there, I thought you were a redhead in hiding," he explained when he realized that his intense curiosity had been too obvious.

Kate frowned and slapped the pith helmet back on her head. "Actually, I was wondering myself why your nickname is Huck when you have Tom Sawyer's red hair." She peered at the dash of pinpoint cinnamon dots sprinkled across his high, wide cheekbones. "And freckles."

He shrugged. "Just one of those things. My name sounds close to Finn, of course, and I grew up mostly in towns along the Mississippi—Twain's Huckleberry country." He plucked a dandelion and stuck the stem between his lips. "And I think I used to run around in dirty overalls and bare feet a lot."

She nodded. "It fits."

"And what about you, teach? Any childhood nicknames?"

"Brain-o-matic," Kate blurted out, picking the least objectionable nickname she'd had to endure.

Jamie was looking at her as closely as she'd examined the tick squirming at the end of her tweezers. She prayed her eyes wouldn't betray her lie of omission. "Also Doc Jr., because both of my parents had Ph.Ds," she added, hurriedly trying to lead him further from the sore subject; there were other nicknames she didn't want to reveal. "Oscar and Sylvia Mallory, semifamous research scientists."

Jamie tossed away the stem he'd been chewing. "Never heard of 'em. But then, I doubt we travel in the same circles."

"They almost won a Nobel prize for their groundbreaking work in symbiotics. They've produced reams of research material and coauthored the definitive book on the subject."

Jamie touched her arm briefly. "But their greatest collaboration was you."

Kate's eyebrows shot up. "That was a nice thing to say, but actually . . . they adopted me. I don't know who my biological parents are. Or were. Whatever." All she knew was that one of them had passed on to her red hair, which had been the bane of her existence until she'd dyed it brown, and that she didn't reveal such intimate details to a mere acquaintance. Flustered, she started gathering up her supplies. "The kids'll be running wild," she explained, reaching for her field guide. "I've got to get back to work."

"They're doing fine," Jamie averred. His daughter was bounding through the forget-me-nots, haplessly but devotedly waving a butterfly net. "Look at Suze. I think you've managed to rouse her intellect, which is a pretty rare occurrence since she launched herself into the boy-crazy years full-force."

"So that's what happened to her," Kate murmured, watching as the bouncy blaze-haired Suzannah dodged past Gregory Gordon Hodge and crashed with a squeal into the chest of a good-looking but thick-headed young athlete who was in summer school to make the grade for the upcoming football season. Though there wasn't a butterfly in sight, Suzannah had apparently netted her trophy.

Kate scolded herself. She should have realized what was going on. Unfortunately, studies had proved that teenage girls still found it necessary to play dumb around their male classmates, and guess who'd been Suzannah's lab partner all of last semester? "I truly am an idiot," Kate said.

Jamie shook his head. "The brilliant Ms. Mallory? Not possible."

"How brilliant can I be when I'd assumed that Suzannah's lack of effort was—" Kate squeezed her eyes shut; she didn't have the guts to look at Jamie as she made her confession. "I thought it was your fault." Squinting, she waved one hand in weak supplication. "You know, the influence of the bar, all that drinking and smoking and lounging about..."

Surprisingly, Jamie chuckled. "I guess I can't really blame you. I am kind of laid-back." He leaned a little closer and lowered his voice. "But I'm not a layabout—unless I've got a partner and the circumstances are, shall we say, optimum."

Kate's eyes opened wide. "Oh!" Her tentative smile wobbled. "I'm not certain I know what you're—"

"Sure you do, teach." Jamie's upper lip was doing its thing and the fine hairs on her nape and forearms were reacting the same way Ben Franklin's must have when he'd flown that kite in the lightning storm. At last she knew the true meaning of the term *charged particles*.

"Be that as it may," she said sternly, doing her best not to give herself away, "I think it's time we reconnoitered with the other chaperons and returned to the campground. I've planned a full agenda for the rest of the day and we mustn't fall behind schedule."

"Run and catch up to Gordon Hodge, then, teach," Jamie called as he followed her at a lazy amble. "He brought along one of those pocket-size Rolodex computers. You two can regulate, collate and cross-reference to your busy little hearts' content."

Kate fled, pretending she hadn't heard. But something was telling her it wouldn't be so easy to outrun herself.

GORDON HODGE had a torchlike gizmo he used to light that night's campfire. Much to Jamie's amusement, he also had a battery-powered insect disposal system—a two-foot-long wand that he valiantly waved at the mosquitoes humming around Kate's head, suctioning them into a sealed car-

tridge lined with a lethal gel. He filled three of the dispos-
able cartridges before giving up and breaking out the old-
fashioned mosquito head nets he'd packed as a last resort.

Armed with bug spray, Kate declined when Gordon gentlemanly offered her his own personal head net. She did give
him points for being prepared and making the attempt, unlike Jamie, who sat on a mossy log slapping mosquitoes and
trading quips with Monica. The traitor.

After they'd all made themselves sick on gooey s'mores
and the kids had tried their best to scare themselves silly
with ghost stories, Kate declared it time to roll out the
sleeping bags. They'd been assigned two of the rustic
campground's permanent sleeping tents, which were nothing more than room-size wooden platforms roofed by
musty canvas sheets. Jamie and Gordon took charge of the
boys; Monica and Kate were bedding down with the six
girls.

Two hours later, Kate had admired Gordon's egg-shaped
ultrasonic contact lens washing machine, interrupted one
teenage rendezvous behind the latrines and assured five
frightened girls that a certain eerie wailing they'd taken for
the dirge of a headless corpse—never mind that if it was
headless it was also mouthless—was only the wind in the
treetops. Monica and her daughter Kirsten slept through it
all.

Once Kate was sure the girls were finally asleep, she quietly dug a beach towel out of her duffel and slipped from the
tent.

The woods were relatively quiet. The dirge was actually
a light sigh of breeze not nearly strong enough to cool Kate's
overheated system. She intended to rendezvous with the
small but deep pond she'd sighted through the thick forest
foliage off one of the main footpaths. The boy's tent was si-

lent as she passed; Kate was quite proud of herself for re-
sisting the temptation to peek inside and check on Jamie.

She was about to veer off the trail in search of the pond
when a rustling movement, followed by a grunt, came from
the underbrush in the opposite direction. Kate's first
thought was of bears. But it was more of a manly grunt, so
her second was of Jamie Flynn. She wasn't sure which species would be more dangerous to her well-being at this
point.

Gordon Hodge emerged from the woods, his sandy
brush-cut hair peppered with bits of dried bark and pine
needles. Kate exhaled with relief. She couldn't imagine
anyone less dangerous than Gordon Hodge wearing a
wraparound terry robe and— "Gordon!" she exclaimed.
"What have you got on your feet?"

Sheepishly he lifted one leg over a crumbling stump and
set his right foot on the trail. The left carefully followed. His
ungainly footgear sloshed; Kate giggled. "Portable heated
foot massagers," Gordon said. He picked up one foot and
wiggled it so it sloshed louder. "A Gordon Hodge Original," he declared proudly.

"How . . . clever."

Gordon beamed. "You see, the polyurethane base is filled
with water." He held out his push-button remote unit. "This
controls the water temperature and the level of the massag-
ing action. I have an AC version, too, but the cordless model
allows for greater freedom of movement." He bent his knees
and jounced up and down in the clownishly large "plat-
form" shoes. "They're really comfortable and soothing after an active day. Want to try them?"

"Maybe another time, thanks."

"Okey-dokey," he said happily. Gordon plodded down
the trail—swish-*plop*, swish-*plop*—then stopped abruptly
and turned back to Kate, saying, "I was wondering if

you—" He was rocking back and forth, having lost his footing inside the slippery shoes. "If—if—y-you—" he stuttered, still teetering, his arms flailing for the pine boughs overhanging the path.

Kate stepped over and wrapped her arms around him from behind, supporting his weight until he found his balance. "Yikes," he said. "Looks like I've still got some tinkering to do."

"Can you make it back to the tent?"

Gordon shuffled forward, the shoes squidging in the muddy puddles of their overflow. "I think so."

Kate bit back a grin. "Be careful."

"You be careful, too," he said, although most of his attention was directed to the business of aiming the remote control at his toes and punching buttons. "I tried a shortcut from the latrines and almost got lost. You'll be better off sticking to the path, Kate."

And staying out of Gordon Hodge Originals, she thought as she watched him fidget with the shoes. Distractedly, he returned to his interrupted question. "I was wondering if— you'd consider going out—" he shook the remote control frantically "—with me—some—time—" Wisps of steam wafted around his ankles.

"Sure, Gordon," she said, and hoped he'd missed her involuntary sigh of resignation. The things she did to fill up her roster of Love Bytes candidates!

When he began to elaborate despite the obviously uncomfortable warmth his foot massagers were generating, she said, "Why don't you call me?"

He hopped up and down like a step-aerobiciser, his robe flapping open to reveal knobby knees and pale hairless thighs. "Yes—I'll call," he said, sketching a hasty wave goodbye and disappearing down the forest trail at a pace too speedy for safety.

So much for midnight encounters in the forest primeval, Kate thought semicheerfully as she detoured around a fragrant balsam fir. It wasn't as if she'd *really* been hoping to run into Jamie....

The way to the pond was carpeted in a fairyland path of silvered lichen and spongy moss. Soon, waist-deep in ferns, Kate came to a lush glade sheltered by towering cedars. The small pond, cupped within a bowl of mossy stones, shimmered like a cut emerald, undisturbed and quietly enchanting in the moonlight.

She kicked off her flip-flops and stepped out of her jeans. Leaving her towel on one of the rocks, she entered the chilly water with a shudder, her bare feet sinking into the muddy bottom. Two steps and she was already waist-deep, her arms stretched before her like the prow of a ship, pleating the still surface into cold satiny ripples.

"Kate Mallory," said a nearby voice, quiet and husky and faintly taunting. "Right now, I'd say you look more like a mermaid than a schoolteacher."

Kate stood stock-still, unafraid, though there was a shiver dancing lightly on her spine.

"So glad I didn't sleep through this," Jamie's voice continued, accompanied by the lap of water against stone and skin as he slipped into the pond.

"You," Kate whispered, turning. Jamie still had one arm draped across a rounded mossy rock, the pose defining the muscles in his bare chest, making it look all the broader. His ruddy hair was tousled and cowlicked, like a naughty boy's. His light hazel eyes glowed even in the deep shadows cast by the cedar trees and his lips beckoned to hers with silent laughter.

Kate's voice caught in her chest for a long moment before she found it again. "You! You, Jamie Flynn, look like— like ... Puck." A quite unscientific image sprang to mind.

"A midnight prankster," she continued, the words that floated out of her mouth seeming to have no connection to the everyday, ever rational Kate Mallory. "Roaming the night bent on all sorts of mischief and mayhem and deviltry."

He threw back his head and laughed. "Sounds like one helluva chaperon."

"I must have been out of my mind to ask you."

He glided to her through the dark green water, as sinuous and silent as a sea serpent. "Which is a good thing, right?" he whispered, boldly rising up out of the water at a point where only inches and her modest tank swimsuit separated them.

"I don't—"

"Come on, Kate. Admit it." He slid his hands around her waist and eased her closer. She felt the cool jet of an underground spring beneath her feet but that didn't stop her tremulous insides from warming as if she'd stepped into a volcano instead. "I sense it in you, you know," Jamie murmured. "The longing to lose your mind . . ."

Closing her eyes, Kate surrendered with a soft moan. Jamie's seductive voice was temptation at its purest. His hard, smooth brown body was the essence of sin. And, even though she'd always worked hard to deny it, he was right about her; she did long to escape—escape herself, most of all—just for a little while. Just to see what it would be like.

Jamie's lips brushed her cheek; it was more of a tease than a kiss. "Don't you ever want to go a little wild?" he whispered.

"I don't," she insisted weakly. How did he *know*?

"Oh, teach." Jamie released her and moved away in a cold swirl of water. Alarmed, Kate opened her eyes and saw that he was just an arm's length away, his face filled with the kind of sensual knowledge that, for her, had always been only another theory. She was a little bit afraid. Which actually felt rather . . . thrilling.

Her body drifted toward his. She stopped it.

He looked at her gravely, shaking his head. "Teach, what you need is a whole new kind of chemistry lesson. And I'm just the man to give it to you."

3

KATE CROSSED HER ARMS, gripping her own shoulders. Holding herself back, Jamie decided. "I do not need a chemistry lesson," she insisted. "Certainly not from—"

"Yes, you do." Instinct told him to wait for her to come to him. Already she was imperceptibly closer, though he hadn't actually seen her move. If he reached out now he could run his fingertip across the wet skin of her raised arms and watch them uncross and fall away, her defenses broached by one simple gesture.

But, no. He could wait.

Kate glanced down. A deep breath shuddered through her. When she looked up again, still only inches away, Jamie waited. Nervously she scanned the dark fringed circle of the cedars and the shadowed fronds shrouding the pond, listened to the deep silence of the forest. No excuses there. No reason to turn back.

Eyes huge, she dropped her arms. The water made silver bracelets around her wrists as she plunged her hands beneath the surface, then back up, splashing water on her face, dampening her hair as she slicked it away from her forehead. "All right," she said, trying to sound challenging even though the level of her voice was scarcely above a whisper. "Kiss me."

As he leaned closer, the corners of his mouth twitched in an attempt to restrain his triumph. Kate's lips were pressed together in a prim line, so instead of kissing them his tongue darted out and caught the droplet of water that had beaded on the end of her nose. Her head jerked; she sucked in a quick, harsh breath.

Jamie smiled. And he waited.

After a long moment, Kate closed her eyes. Her lips had softened. She made a tiny, welcoming gesture, tilting her head just so. Electricity prickled through the hair at Jamie's nape. He was inclined to make her wait even longer, maybe see if she'd ask him again, but found he didn't have the willpower to prolong this torture. Tasting Kate was a temptation he could no longer resist.

He put his mouth to hers. With a small, sliding adjustment, they fit together perfectly, his curved upper lip melding with the lushness of her bottom lip as he nibbled it delicately, slipping his tongue over it in a way that drew from her a deep, soulful sigh.

He brushed his fingers over her bare shoulders, reaching up to tangle them in her hair as Kate tilted her head back. Her lips parted and he felt the involuntary quiver of her velvet tongue against his, the accompanying shiver of her body as he pressed his advantage. The water swirled around their joined bodies like iced satin, an exquisite contrast to the warm need pulsing between them.

Kate wrenched her head away. "D-don't you think that's enough?" Her pupils had expanded like blots of ink in the glimmering pools of her green irises.

"Since you gave me the choice, my answer would have to be no." Jamie advanced as she backpedaled toward the rocks, their feet squelching in the muck. "Hmm, bad choice of phrasing for a schoolteacher—unless it was on purpose?" His eyebrows peaked devilishly.

He'd flustered her. "No. Umm, I mean, I don't know."

His hands had slipped to her waist; he linked them at the small of her back to keep her from getting away. "I know," he said distinctly, separating the words so they sounded implacably wise.

Kate's hands sneaked up between their bodies, making the muscles in his abdomen contract under her touch. He crushed her to him for another kiss. She succumbed with only a halfhearted wiggle of her palms against his pebbled nipples, then a last-ditch sideways swoop of her head. His mouth landed on her shoulder; he chuckled in his throat and took the opportunity to taste the soft, damp flesh cut by the strap of her swimsuit. He caught the strap between his teeth and, stretching the fabric tight as his eyes flashed on hers, peeled it down her bicep.

Her hands fluttered up to shield the slope of her cleavage. "Please..."

"Since you asked so nicely..." He unlinked his fingers, then, bumping hers away, he inserted both his hands inside the neckline of the suit and slowly rolled it down over her full breasts, his cold wet palms pressed tightly to their outer curves. Her nipples popped out, flushed and hard as pink diamonds.

Kate's arousal was threaded with perplexed distress. Seeing this, Jamie returned to her lips, coaxing her with kisses and soothing murmurs until she melted against him, returning his passion in full, answering his caresses with her own tentative forays across his broad shoulders. Her mouth was sublime. His breath grew ragged with the need for more.

And when it came again, Kate's purred "Oh, please, Jamie..." was an invitation.

He bracketed her breasts with his wet hands, lifting them so their taut peaks traced burning pinpoints of fire across his chest. Kate arched her spine, her shoulder blades scraping the large craggy rock behind her. As she stretched her arms overhead to find a handhold on the mossy granite, her out-thrust breasts swayed temptingly. Agonized, Jamie struggled with the urge to take her then and there—no gentlemanly restraint, only savage intensity. But he knew Kate would soon regret such a coupling, and he knew he couldn't bear to be the instigator of her shame.

Neither was he noble enough to stop. Not yet. Not when she was spread before him like a pagan goddess, the moonlight spilling over her ivory breasts. Her swimsuit was puddled beneath her expanding and contracting rib cage, where the pond lapped at her waist. The water churned as he wrapped his hands around her hips, lifting her even higher. His mouth was hot on her lush breasts. She moaned his name and twined her legs around his hips, bringing their pelvises into intimate alignment. His throbbing erection was trapped beneath the heavy wet fabric of his trunks. Wantonly Kate tilted her hips and pressed against it, giving him a sample of how frustrating teasing could be.

Her flesh tasted like musky woman and lake water. Like starlight and secrets. Aching to devour her, he feasted instead, making her undulate beneath the lashings of his tongue. A breeze set the branches of the cedars bobbing, casting feathery shadows across Kate's closed eyelids, her extended arms and pale, silvered torso.

Jamie raised his head, pausing with the fingernail of his thumb grazing one of her swollen nipples. This was dangerous, very dangerous. Dangerous in any number of ways. They couldn't go on. But could he make himself stop?

A sudden thrashing in the woods broke through Kate's sex-drugged mind. Gasping, visibly stricken, she thrust herself away from Jamie, frantically pulling at her swimsuit as she sank until the water was up to her shoulders. Turning her back to him, bowing her head, she pulled the straps up her arms.

The rustling sounds faded deeper into the forest. "It's okay." Jamie's voice was hoarse. "Probably just an animal. It's gone now."

"Probably?" Kate repeated, aghast. "But maybe not?"

"No, I'm sure it was a wild animal."

She put her face in her hands. "What if someone saw us? What in the world did I think I was doing?"

"You were—"

"No! Don't say it!" She scrambled up the steep bank, water sluicing from her limbs. Hunching to shield herself from his gaze, she averted her face behind the dripping curtain of her hair and quickly wrapped the towel beneath her arms. "How could I?" she muttered under her breath, then rounded on Jamie, her hands in fists. She stamped her bare foot. "How could you do that to me?"

He stepped back, his spirits sinking lower than the mud sucking at his ankles. There it was, in Kate's white face, her hollow eyes: embarrassment and shame.

So soon, dammit. And, if the truth be known, so inevitable.

We did it to each other, part of him wanted to say. "I shouldn't have," he answered instead, shouldering all of the responsibility. "I apologize."

"It was entirely inappropriate." Kate bent, then straightened, clutching her jeans to her chest. "I could be fired for this. And I'd deserve it."

"Oh, come on, now, Kate, don't blame yourself—"

"No. I knew what kind of man you were. And still I stayed. I was the one who asked you to chaperon. This is all my fault."

What type? Jamie figured it wouldn't be flattering but probably no worse than he'd called himself. "No one's getting fired for a little harmless kissing."

"It was more than kissing. A lot more." Color rising in her cheeks, her eyes slammed shut. "I did things . . . I must have been out of my mind . . . I was . . . I was out of my mind." She spoke through clenched teeth, and then her eyes opened to burn like lasers into his. "Don't you get it?" she seethed. Her voice dropping, she added, "I wasn't going to stop."

Gooseflesh corrugated Jamie's skin. Yet, after a tense moment, he found his cocky grin, a shrug. "You say that like it's a bad thing."

Kate made a screeching sound of frustration and turned away. She whipped past a pungent cedar and stomped through the ferns, disappearing into the dark forest without another word. She was one extremely pissed-off mermaid.

With reason, Jamie acknowledged bleakly. Disgusted with himself, he drove his fingers into his hair, yanking it by the roots. Which reminded him of Kate, of her habit of fussily smoothing her hair at moments of distress. His hands plopped into the pond like stones.

He'd pushed her too far, too fast. She'd shocked herself. Hell, she'd shocked him. He'd had a sneaking suspicion that she was hiding a passionate streak, but to have it explode into a fireball in his very hands had been more than he'd expected.

Kate was more than he'd expected. She was an intoxicating, addictive enigma. Already he craved another taste of her.

Of course, he'd blown any chance of that by his flippant response to what had been her stark admission: *I wasn't going to stop.* She wasn't, she couldn't, until he'd given her good reason to run as fast as she could away from him. Right now, she was probably berating herself for associating with someone so beneath her, no matter how hot their chemistry.

Jamie collapsed backward in the green water, plunging deep, then reaching up with his head, teeth bared, as he rose back to the surface in a spread-eagled float. Sharp stars pricked the night sky with their brilliance. The tension in his body was slowly soothed by the cool water, but its ravening hunger would not dissipate so easily.

"SOMETHING BIG HAPPENED," Monica said. Her dark eyes were avid. "Why won't you tell me what it was?"

Standing at the bathroom sink, Kate tugged her narrow linen-covered belt in a notch. Had she lost that much weight? In the four days since she'd made such a fool of herself with Jamie, she'd had no appetite at all. And she'd thought she'd been feeling out of sorts before!

"It was just a mistake, that's all." Kate had been too alarmed at the emergence of her wild and wanton self to tell even Monica about the encounter with Jamie. It was best forgotten. Or at least ignored.

"More than a mistake," Monica insisted from the bedroom. "I can tell when you're thinking about it, you know. You get a tiny horizontal crease between your eyebrows, your eyes go all hazy and then you blush. See . . . you're doing it again!"

Kate frowned at her pink cheeks in the mirror. "That's just makeup." Calmly she combed her hair and clipped it at the back of her neck with a gold barrette. In her simple white-collared navy dress, opaque hose and matching two-tone pumps, she looked dull but presentable. There'd be no overactive libidos on this date.

"Yup," Monica snorted, sitting cross-legged on the bed. "Just makeup."

"All right, all right, I give up." Kate spun on her heel to face her relentlessly curious neighbor. "Jamie and I kissed."

"And?"

"And tonight I have a date."

Exasperated, Monica tossed her hands in the air. "With Gordon Hodge!"

"Gordon is a nice, respectable man. If all goes well on our date, I'm going to make him a candidate for Love Bytes. He might be exactly the type who'd make me a very suitable husband. Most women would overlook him."

"If suitable is all you want in a husband, you may as well save yourself the trouble and elope with Mr. Buntz."

Kate stood in the doorway between the rooms. "Mr. Buntz!"

Monica shrugged. "He's quiet and unobtrusive. He has an IRA and a pension. Best of all, he's right next door. You could live side by side and never be bothered with anything unseemly like belching, dirty socks and morning breath. Considering his age, you probably wouldn't even be subjected to those nasty, messy conjugal rights most husbands demand—the rutting beasts. Plus you'd get Boris."

"Is that supposed to make me laugh?"

"Only if you've *really* entered Mr. Buntz into Love Bytes."

"Of course not." Kate paused. "But how big is that pension, now that you mention it?"

She did laugh then, but it was a subdued chuckle. Not enough time had passed to allow her to hear the word *rutting* without thinking of . . . Her eyes lost their focus.

"How did Love Bytes rate Jamie's kiss?" Monica asked craftily.

Kate blinked. "I'm not including him in the program," she said briskly, bustling around the room without a legitimate purpose. She was pretending to herself that she was looking for her purse, even though it was on the bed in full view.

"Afraid?"

Kate's head snapped up. "Of what?"

Monica grinned. "You tell me."

"There's no point to it. Jamie Flynn is just not...viable."

"Did you say *vital*?"

"I did not."

"*Virile*?"

"Shut up, Monica."

GORDON HODGE took Kate to a midpriced family restaurant. They ate shrimp and fish and talked about current events, the weather and the progress of the Green Bay Packers training camp. It was all very civilized.

They went to a movie with no excessive violence or sex. Kate had trouble keeping her attention focused on the screen. Oblivious, Gordon munched unbuttered popcorn and laughed in all the right places.

Afterward, they stopped for coffee. Decaffeinated. Kate asked Gordon about his career and forced herself to listen to his discourse on mechanical engineering at the Magnatech Corporation. At the back of her mind she kept a running tab for Love Bytes. Gordon would do well in most of the categories. Maybe even well enough to top her present roster, along with the professor she'd been seeing off and on. Which said more about the other candidates than it did about Gordon. By the time they arrived back at her house, Kate was downcast, but she wasn't blaming Gordon.

She was blaming Jamie.

Had he ruined her for ordinary men?

"Tinkering with my projects is just a sideline," Gordon was saying in response to her question about the progress of the foot massagers. He chuckled. "I may be a crazy inventor, but not crazy enough to think I'd make a living at it." His Love Bytes Practicality score soared.

She had to stop thinking about Jamie. Gordon deserved a fighting chance. Kate opened her gate and invited him through. By the light of the coach lantern at her door, she concentrated on his face. He had even features, mild brown eyes, a close shave. Moderately applied cologne. His suit and tie were classic, clean and unwrinkled. He probably changed his socks twice a day and she couldn't imagine him doing anything as impolite as belching. Conjugal relations with someone like Gordon could be pleasant and most likely not particularly demanding. He was her perfect Love Bytes match in many ways. *So there, Monica!*

"Thank you, Gordon," she said. "I had a very nice time."

He smiled. "So did I, Kate."

She wondered if she should invite him in to test out how he'd score on those "less important" Sexual Attraction categories.

"I'll leave you here, then," Gordon said before Kate could bring herself to do it. His gaze shifted from her face to a spot over her right shoulder. He cleared his throat. "May I kiss you goodnight?"

Kate's grip on her clutch purse relaxed. Mentally she nudged Gordon's Etiquette score up a notch and lifted her face to his. "Yes, you may, Gordon," she said with cool detachment.

Although not disagreeable, Gordon's kiss was as bland as the man. Kate's Physical Response-Female score didn't so much as jitter.

Gordon looked happy. He said goodbye and made his way through her yard with a certain jauntiness to his step, swinging through the gate without even remembering to close it behind him.

Sighing, Kate let herself droop, thunking her head on the front door a bit harder than she'd intended. Maybe she needed a good knock on the noggin to jolt the appropriate response out of her. Gordon Hodge was suitable—eminently suitable. Love Bytes was sure to agree.

A soft, insinuating voice carried through the garden: "Nice, Kate. *Very* nice." It was followed by a curiously familiar clicking.

"Who's there?" Kate demanded, but judging by the sudden spiking of her senses she already knew. A beat later the clicking sounds registered. She was tempted to keep quiet about them and let Jamie suffer the consequences.

A low, menacing growl changed her mind. "Watch out for the dog," she shouted toward wherever Jamie was hiding in the dark jungle of shrubbery as she lunged for the stone path. "Boris! Come here, Boris! No, Boris! Bad dog!"

Mr. Buntz's boxer had plunged into the garden, growling and barking. Kate gave chase, batting at the foliage with her purse. "Heel, Boris," she commanded uselessly, expecting to hear Jamie's howl of pain at any moment. With the exception of Mr. Buntz, Boris had a notorious hatred of men. The mail carrier and Ed Danielson bore the teethmarks to prove it. She crashed through a four-foot-high clump of goldenrod and skidded to a stop.

Jamie was kneeling beneath the crab apple tree, his hand at the back of Boris's neck, twisting his studded collar tight enough to hold him in place. The dog was waggling his stumpy tail and making conciliatory whimpers. Jamie let Boris sniff his hand.

"Get the gate," he said to the tongue-tied Kate. Crouching, he walked Boris through the garden and along the cobbled path. He released him on the sidewalk, nimbly stepped aside, and Kate slammed the twig gate shut. The humiliated Boris yapped halfheartedly, then trotted toward home, his hind end twitching.

Kate slowly turned to face Jamie. She flinched when he picked a twig out of her hair. *As if he intended to throw you to the ground and ravish you right there,* she scoffed at herself. *Really, Kate.*

"So," she accused in retaliation for her unruly thoughts, "you were spying on me." And he'd seen her kiss Gordon Hodge! She wished she'd given it more of an effort.

"I didn't mean to spy. I was simply sitting under the apple tree, waiting for you to come home."

Was his grin sly? Did he think her amusing? Kate grunted. "Do you always make calls at such unconventional times?"

"My schedule . . ." He shrugged. "I'm a night person."

"I'm a morning person," she retorted. She was feeling churlish. Badly out of sorts. And more alive than she'd been for the past four days.

Jamie brushed a few leaves off her shoulders. She managed not to flinch. "What's up with your yard anyway?" he asked.

"It's not a yard. It's a wildlife habitat." Knowing he would follow, she walked back toward the house without issuing an invitation. "Butterfly weed," she said, pointing to the orange flowers that grew beside the path. "*Asclepias tuberosa*. And this is common milkweed, food for the larvae of monarch butterflies. It's toxic to anyone else."

"Keen."

"That was the general attitude of the thirteen-year-olds in my natural science class," Kate said. They'd reached her front door. On the other side was safety—and the lifetime of moderation she'd been trained by her parents to accept without question.

"I like it when you lecture me like a schoolmarm," Jamie said huskily. "For some strange reason, it turns me on."

She frowned, her nerve endings buzzing. "I was going for the opposite effect."

His eyes glinted. "Now you know."

"I won't try it again," she whispered, knowing nothing, not when he was looking at her that way. Her learned patterns of acceptable behavior had vanished. The security of inhibition was gone. All that kept her out of Jamie's arms were her petrified feet.

"Can I have another chance with you?" he asked.

Kate's throat constricted. She knew she should say no, but at the moment that was impossible. She was bursting with *yes,* even if she couldn't articulate it. Finally she nodded.

Jamie's relief and pleasure were evident. Kate hadn't stopped to think about what he was feeling for her. Now she wondered. Did he find her attractive? Recalling the incident in the pond she decided he must. At least in the dark. What, then, had he thought when she'd kissed him like a wild woman and then bolted?

Did he want only a physical relationship?

Did *she?*

Kate's circumscribed behavior had worked like a charm on most of the men she'd known. There'd been a few skirmishes on sofas and back seats, but usually her dates had acted as gentlemen once she'd made it clear that she expected no less. Her few serious relationships had been with nice, bland men like Gordon Hodge. Before Jamie, it hadn't occurred to her that she might actually want a different type. Simply for the opportunity to experience what exactly all the hullabaloo about infatuation and lust was about.

But it would definitely not have any relevance to Love Bytes.

"I promise not to step out of bounds again," he said.

Kate's expectations crumbled. "You do?"

"That's what you want, right?"

"Er, well, I . . ."

"At least not on our first date," he added with a curl of his quirky upper lip.

IT TURNED OUT THAT Jamie was a man true to his word.

Two days later, he took Kate all the way to Green Bay to watch the Packers scrimmage with the New Orleans Saints, one of the unofficial Cheese League of teams who held training camps in Wisconsin. Although Kate had learned to enjoy a good NFL game on occasion, it was an outing she thought slightly strange—it wasn't like a scrimmage was an actual game, even an exhibition game—but a couple of thousand people apparently were just as crazy as Jamie.

The bleachers at the practice field were jam-packed with fans. Green-and-gold Packers regalia ruled the day. Jamie bought Kate the de rigueur cheesehead, so she spent the afternoon wearing a foam block of cheddar on her head. It was quite a fashion statement, especially in eighty-five degree weather.

"Don't tell me you're one of those," she said to Jamie once the scrimmage had ended and the crowd was thinning out. Many of the fans had clustered at the chain-link fence to get autographs from the players.

"A cheesehead?"

"A Packers fanatic. Or is it the same thing?"

Jamie laughed, plucked the cheddar off her head and plopped it on his instead. On him, it worked—absurdly. "No," he answered, "a cheesehead can be a Bucks, Brewers and Badgers fanatic, too."

"Are you?" Kate asked with suspicion. She hadn't thought to include such variables in her computer program. Would she end up with one of those husbands who spent every weekend in front of the TV? Like Monica's Ed?

"On occasion," Jamie admitted.

She'd been a Wisconsinite long enough to know that *fanatic* and *on occasion* were mutually exclusive words, but she didn't call him on it. After all, he wasn't a part of Love Bytes.

Not yet. She followed him to his Jeep, circa 1989, open-topped and sporting several dings and rust spots.

Several miles out of Green Bay, Kate's thoughts turned to her placid dinner date with Gordon Hodge, a man she hadn't hesitated to include in Love Bytes. While Gordon had simply spoken of the Packers' preseason training camp, Jamie had driven one hundred miles to participate as a fan. He had cheered, booed, laughed, groaned, hooted and hollered. He'd had fun. She had, too, now that she thought about it, although the moves that lingered in her mind were not those that had taken place on the football field. She'd savored Jamie's every hug, smack on the cheek and hand-holding, even if they were just an overflow of his enthusiasm for the football game.

He wasn't content to merely observe life. He lived it full out.

Whereas, Kate realized, she, even more than Gordon, was strictly an observer. She was a teacher, not a doer. Take her out of the classroom and put her outdoors and she became a bird watcher, note taker and specimen gatherer. She collected, categorized and studied.

On the whole, her leisure time occupations were also nonparticipatory. She bought tickets to Belle Terre's symphony series every winter, attended the Music in the Park concerts in the summer. She chaperoned school dances from the sidelines. She read biographies about other people's lives and adventures and accomplishments. She did participate in weddings—as a bridesmaid. Perhaps she should take more than a chemistry lesson from Jamie.

Her brow furrowed as they sped along US 41, the jeep rattling. Sophie B. Hawkins was wailing "Damn I Wish I Was Your Lover" on the radio and Jamie was whistling, one hand on the steering wheel, the other bare brown arm propped on the door, his elbow hanging in the wind.

She tried to remember if she'd always been only an observer. There were some vague memories of her early childhood, around ages five, six, seven. She'd run, skipped, climbed trees, sang and laughed at the top of her lungs. In fact, Oscar and Sylvia Mallory had often despaired over their adopted daughter's excessive energy. Was that when she'd changed? Or was it a few years later, when she'd grown so homely and awkward and had gained the nicknames that still made her cringe?

"What do you say to ribs?" Jamie asked.

Kate snapped to. He was steering the car off the highway and into the blacktop parking lot of a joint called Adam's Rib.

She hesitated. Ribs were so messy. She'd get barbecue sauce all over her chin and look like a total slob on their first—or second—date. On the other hand ribs were what could be called a participatory meal. A very small start, but why not?

"Ribs?" she said. "Well, yes, ribs. Lots of them. The messier the better. Why not?"

"Why not?" Jamie agreed. "That's always been my credo."

"I would expect so," she muttered with some irony as they stepped from the car.

The restaurant was rustic, noisy and filled with the spicy scent of roasting meat. Jamie and Kate snagged a table for two on the other side of the salad bar. They ordered ribs, cole slaw, onion rings, corn on the cob. Kate passed up beer for lemonade and asked for extra paper napkins.

"You were looking very thoughtful before, in the Jeep," Jamie said. She'd been frowning, actually, and he'd been disappointed. He'd thought she'd enjoyed the football scrimmage, even if it wasn't something she'd ordinarily do.

"I was thinking about how, when I was a child, I was more like you." She slowly rolled her bottom lip between her teeth, then shrugged. "Somewhere along the way, I changed. I can't seem to remember exactly when."

"Are you saying I'm childish?" he gibed.

"Not exactly. I was referring to the way you enjoy life. It makes me seem dull in contrast."

Jamie tried to withhold his mischievous grin. Earnest Kate was so much fun to tease. "I wouldn't use the word *dull* for a woman who transforms into a mermaid at midnight. You should come with directions—Just Add Water. Don't tell me you've already forgotten . . . ?" It was a sight he'd relish all his life: Kate, halfnaked and voluptuous, her deep green eyes unfathomable with passion, erotic fuel for a zillion fantasies. He sustained little hope for the real hands-on version.

She was blushing; her reddish lashes lowered as she looked down at the knotty pine tabletop. "You promised you wouldn't go out of bounds again," she said in a husky voice. That did dastardly things to his resolution not to tempt either of them too far.

"Hey, I've been very good up to now, haven't I? Notice how it's broad daylight and we're out in public. This date's been strictly platonic." Save a few overzealous squeezes he'd excused under the guise of football fervor.

She chose not to wander down that particular conversational path. "All right, then, if I'm not dull, can we agree that I'm too serious?"

"Whatever you say, teach," he drawled.

"Precisely."

Jamie could tell that she was trying to figure something out. "If that's your natural inclination . . ." he suggested, letting her supply the rest. Personally, he had his doubts.

"The braces?" Kate muttered to herself. "The growth spurt? The freckles, the hair?"

"Pardon? Did you say freckles?"

She shook her head and deliberately threw him off the scent. "My parents were awfully serious. They'd set up a home laboratory, and they claimed too much noise and activity in the house disturbed their concentration. My father often scolded me for being rambunctious, as he called it. Said he didn't believe in allowing even a child to indulge in bad behavior."

"So there's your answer," Jamie said. A waitress was coming toward their table with an overloaded tray. Kate inclined her head. She did have tiny freckles, he saw. Not many, maybe only as a result of that day's exposure to the sun.

"I'll bet you were allowed to be as rambunctious as you pleased," she said, looking achingly lovely and natural with her sun-kissed cheeks and bare lips, her shining brown hair spread across her shoulders.

The waitress arrived. "Yeah," Jamie said, "and that explains a lot about me, too." Dishes were plunked onto the table until the surface was too crowded for his elbows. He picked up a dinner roll and tore it in half. Kate was peeling open one of the paper napkins, staring at her plate with a daunted expression. "Dig in," he suggested. "I promise not to report you for bad behavior."

Suddenly hungry, Kate smiled and picked up a gloppy hunk of the spareribs with her fingers.

THAT EVENING, Kate was still staring at a screenful of Love Bytes statistics long after she'd finished the file on subject #34GH, a.k.a. Gordon Hodge. As suspected, he earned high marks in many of the categories. She'd left the Sexual Attraction scores open for now, seeing as how there was more research to do. Once Jamie had been worked out of her noncomputer system, she could give Gordon another chance.

She had to keep reminding herself that he was a very nice man.

So was Jamie, after a fashion. He'd returned Kate to her house intact, her virtue unimpeached. As promised, he hadn't even tried for so much as a kiss.

Darn it anyway.

Then she started thinking . . . Supposedly she was egalitarian. She'd worked up stats on almost every other eligible male she'd met, including those who didn't have a snowball's chance of being selected, like Rodney Pfaeffle.

How could she consider Rod a candidate and not Jamie?

It was amateurishly subjective to resist.

And, anyway, it wasn't as if he'd end up being her perfect match.

Slowly, with one finger, Kate pecked at the keyboard. #35JF—Jamie Flynn.

Strictly for the sake of her data base.

4

THE SUN WAS HIGH, hot and hard. Kate was wearing a red bandanna, gypsy-style, a large straw hat and SPF 50. She still had a redhead's delicate skin even though her hair had been brown for the past sixteen years.

Jamie, an unregenerate redhead, wasn't so afflicted. He was tanned all over, wearing a purple-black Huckleberries T-shirt and denim cutoffs to her own long-sleeved white blouse and baggy chinos. In the past hour Kate had discovered that she'd never before truly appreciated the beauty of the male leg. Jamie's were long, strong, brown and lightly dusted with springy auburn hair. His muscles flexed impressively when he knelt and lengthened admirably when he stretched. It hadn't taken Kate long to decide that if Jamie was a breast man as she suspected, then she could be a leg woman.

She smiled a secret smile. *Why not?*

They were picking huckleberries at Whistler and Charity's homestead in the countryside fifteen miles out of Belle Terre. The bushes grew thick on the edge of a stand of jack pine, with clusters of purple-black berries weighing down the branches. The warm air hummed with the drone of insects and honeybees; in counterpoint was the trill of chirping sparrows and the thunk of the ripe fruit in their metal pails.

Kate paused to wipe at the sweat stinging her eyes. She was so hot, almost dizzy, and her stomach felt as hollow as a kettledrum. Participatory activities were tougher than she'd thought, even when one took time out for leg watching.

Jamie looked up. "Too hot for you?"

"I'm fine," Kate said, and plopped down into the grass, just managing to keep her berry pail from tipping over.

Jamie was kneeling at her side before she could blink. Clucking in consolation, he tipped off her hat and peeled the bandanna from her head. After dousing it with his water bottle, he used the wet rag to wipe her pink face, his palm gentle under her chin.

He offered her the bottle. "Better?"

Embarrassed, she nodded and drank. The water was warm, but delicious. Some of it trickled down her chin and Jamie wiped it away with a lingering thumb. His knuckles brushed her jaw. Their gazes connected and the moment was ripe with meaning, until the chatter of a nearby chipmunk broke the spell. "I really am fine," Kate insisted, though now her relatively unimpeached virtue was shaky.

He brought over the other berry bucket and picked up hers. "It'll only take me a few minutes to top this one off. Relax, okay? Don't move."

"Okay." She fanned her face with the straw hat and focused on Jamie's tin pail, mounded with juicy huckleberries. It was like a treasure chest spilling over with gleaming purple jewels. She lifted a small handful to her mouth. The berries were soft and sunwarmed, their taste wild and sweet—unlike anything a supermarket could offer. She was filled with swoony sentiment, almost all of it directed toward Jamie. One thoughtful gesture and she turned to syrup. Heavens, but she was a weak woman!

When Kate wasn't watching Jamie, he was sneaking glances at her through the screen of green leaves. She looked soporific, her eyelids drooping, sunshine bringing out the soft red sheen of her hair. Damp strands curled around her flushed cheeks.

He dropped another handful of berries into the pail, then did a doubletake. "Your hair *is* red."

"Mummmph." Her hands fluttered over it.

Curious, he went over and dropped to his knees in front of her. From the temple down, Kate's hair was mainly brown; only the upper third was streaked the red-blond of a half-ripe strawberry. She tried to put her hat back on but he stopped her. "Red like a strawberry?" he said slowly. "Like a strawberry margarita?"

With a reluctant nod, she confessed. "'Strawberry' was one of my nicknames. That and 'Big Red.' I wasn't sure which I hated more."

"Aw, poor Kate," he murmured with a hint of a smile. "Strawberry I get, but why Big Red?"

"I had an early growth spurt. I was taller and clumsier than most of the boys. Not to mention my braces and freckles and knobby knees. You know how kids tease each other. I was too shy to stand up for myself." She said all of this in a breathless rush, as though the words were burning her tongue. She was hugging her knees, her eyes dark with the memory of hurt feelings and self-consciousness.

Jamie fingered a strand of her hair. "But why color it now? You're so beautiful."

"I'm certainly not beautiful!" she protested.

He tilted his head, wondering what she saw when she looked in the mirror. Somewhere along the line, she'd become absolutely gorgeous in his eyes. "Well, red hair actually has little to do with it, either way."

"I know that. Logically."

"Ah. I see."

"Redheads are usually perky, energetic, fiery, cute. None of those words describe me. I'm not a redhead at heart."

Jamie smiled. "Are you sure?"

She bit her lip. "I've never drunk a strawberry margarita in my life."

"Aw, poor Kate," he repeated playfully. "You don't know what you're missing."

"I guess I am a white wine spritzer, after all."

Not at heart—where it counts, he thought, but saved that revelation for later. Kate would learn. He'd already given her an A in Chemistry 101.

Jamie rose, then took Kate's hand to help her up. "I guess this means you hate the color of my hair, too."

Her quick inhale carried a touch of guilt. "I'm not that stupid. At least not for long. Red hair looks good on you, Jamie. You have the personality to carry it off."

"Is it possible that your thinking's a little screwy on this subject?" he suggested as they started walking back to the house, the strong early August sunshine pelting the top of their heads. Kate dropped her hat over Jamie's hair and tied the damp bandanna around hers.

"Since I was adopted, my parents sometimes used to wonder aloud where I'd gotten my red hair. Eventually I came to think of it as the manifestation of all that was wrong with me, all that made me different from my new parents." She looked thoughtful. "I have a regular, standing appointment at a hair salon, and I've gone for years as a matter of course without really thinking about why. But I missed a touch-up appointment last month, for some reason or other, so the original red has been growing out this summer."

Jamie squeezed her hand. "I like it."

"Well, sure. You would."

"Don't think I didn't get my share of teasing as a kid," he said. "Probably every redhead on earth has been called Red."

"It didn't bother you?"

"I had worse things to think about. Harmless name calling was small potatoes."

"Of course you're right. I really have nothing to complain about." Kate paused. "So what was worse, for you?"

Jamie squinted at Whistler and Charity's house, a rough-hewn, handcrafted hodgepodge surrounded by ivied trellises and a pergola of grape vines, set in a small green valley populated with sugar maples, silver birches and bushy evergreens. He'd always thought the house, with its curved cedar shake roof and wide eaves, looked like a cluster of toadstools, sprung from the forest floor as if it had grown there naturally. It was one of his favorite places on earth, the first real home he'd ever known. As a child, the so-called homes he'd shared with his mother had actually been an endless series of rented rooms. Back then, "temporary" had been the only permanent part of his life.

"Jamie?" Kate murmured, tugging on his hand.

He remembered her question. "Being called a bastard," he said bluntly, knowing it was true.

"What!"

"Hey, that's what illegitimate kids were called in a less politically correct time."

"Jamie..." Kate said with uncertainty and concern. "Well, then, I might be one, too, for all I know of my birth parents." She hesitated over the word, then spat it out. "A bastard."

Jamie raised their knotted hands like a winning prize-fighter. "Redheaded bastards of the world unite!"

Kate gulped back a laugh. "Jamie!"

Stepping closer, he swung her arm down again. "Jeez, I hope we don't have the same father. It's obvious there was at least one redheaded hell-raiser procreating throughout the Midwest thirty-some years ago."

Her eyes widened. "I'm sure that's beyond the realm of possibility. Statistically speaking, the odds are incredi—"

"Don't worry," he said when he saw she was taking his little joke seriously. "I got my red hair from my mother."

"You're always making fun of things," Kate reproached. "I believe you have an avoidance compulsion."

"So, this isn't my favorite subject." He dropped her hand and shaded his eyes, looking toward the house. "There's Suze. Charity's got her doing chores, which is more than I accomplish."

"All right," conceded Kate as they started down the sloping hillside to the yard where Jamie's daughter was hanging towels and sheets on the outdoor clothesline, "I'll let you get away with distracting me this time. But don't think the subject's closed. I want to know everything about you for my—" She stopped abruptly. "Because I—"

Jamie thought Kate looked oddly disconcerted. "Because you what?" he asked.

She shrugged, her grip on the bucket handle tightening. "Just because."

Jamie took the pail from her, coming in low and planting a quick kiss on her unsuspecting lips. "Maybe because you like me?"

"Yes," she whispered with solemn reverence.

Balancing buckets, he loped down the hillside, shouting back at her, "Then say it like you mean it."

Laughing, she chased him into the yard, where there was no longer any sign of Suzannah except for an empty basket and wet laundry flapping in the breeze. Jamie set the pails on the back step and went to prime the old-fashioned pump that stood halfway between the house and the barn. Although Charity and Whistler now had running water and solar- and wind-generated energy, there'd been a time when the outdoor pump had supplied the household.

Pure, ice-cold water gushed from the cast iron spout into
the trough below as Jamie worked the handle. "Dive in," he
urged. Kate splashed a little water on her wrists and dabbed
some on her warm cheeks.

"Let me show you." He pumped harder, then stuck his
head under the spout, soaking his hair, his mouth open to
gulp mouthfuls of the chilly water.

Smiling, Kate caught the handle and pumped it up and
down, throwing all her weight into it. Jamie shrugged out
of his T-shirt and happily splashed about, gasping and
hooting as the cold water flowed over him and raised goose
bumps on his skin.

"That's how you do it," he said finally to Kate, taking
back the handle. "It feels great."

Her eyes traced the contours of his chest, then back up to
his dripping hair. "Well, you look like a half-drowned Irish
retriever, but . . . okay." She discarded the bandanna and
rolled up her sleeves. With dubious regard, she toed off her
sneakers, then daintily stepped her bare feet into the muddy
patch around the trough. Jamie pumped strenuously.

Kate thrust her hands under the gushing water. It did feel
deliciously cold. She splashed her hot face once, then several times. It was refreshing, and the back of her neck *was*
hot and sticky with perspiration. . . . She dove in with more
enthusiasm.

When she emerged, slicking her hair back from her forehead, she was as wet but not as bare as Jamie. His gaze lingered on the places where her cotton shirt clung to her
curves. She felt the look as a touch, even hotter than the sun.
Shyly she turned away, the warm mud squidging between
her toes. Her saving grace. "Goodness, now my feet are
rather dirty," she said, purposely putting a touch of the
schoolmarm in her tone.

To Kate's surprise, Jamie pumped the handle, then picked her up. "Stick them under the spout," he said, supporting her weight on his thigh, his foot propped on the trough.

"But—" She lurched with awkward temerity, then wrapped her arms around his shoulders as the cold water splashed over her toes.

Once her feet were clean Jamie switched positions, holding her body to his lengthwise, his hands at her waist. It was a more intimate position than cradling, and Kate had nowhere to look but into his eyes as he carried her, legs dangling, over to the narrow mossy verge that was Whistler's version of a lawn. Except for her hammering pulse, Kate kept still. Not being a petite baby-doll of a woman, she'd never been carried by a man. She was too tall. Too aloof. She hadn't squealed, wiggled or cooed since she was a baby.

Finally she cleared her throat and managed to croak, "You may put me down now, thank you very much."

Jamie loosened his grip only enough for her to slide down an inch, creating a moment of exquisite friction. She stood *en pointe* like a ballerina, still pressed against him. "You may—"

"Kiss you?" he interrupted. "Just once?" His his eyes were incandescent with heated emotion. Kate melted inside.

"I was going to say 'release me,' but, perhaps—" Her shrug was more of a shimmy since she was clasped to his chest "—we can try it your way."

Jamie winked. "How generous of you."

It was a small kiss, a kiss of tantalizing promise, sweet as wild fruit, redolent of the wind, warmed by the sun. When Kate's soft sigh parted her lips enticingly, Jamie's tongue flicked lightly between them, but he did not delve more deeply. His restraint was impressive. And not particularly wanted.

She threaded her fingers through the damp auburn feathers of his long hair and deepened the kiss herself until their mouths hummed with the wonder of it. Despite the desire shimmering between them, Kate pulled back a hairbreadth, her eyes trained on his with steady resolve. "*One* kiss," she whispered, and forced herself to step away.

"Only a schoolteacher would keep so strict a count," Jamie bantered, though he, too, suddenly busied himself retrieving their scattered belongings and carrying the buckets of huckleberries inside.

Only a bartender's kiss would be so intoxicating, Kate thought. And so disturbing. She licked her bottom lip, where his essence seemed to linger. Perhaps a new top score on Love Bytes' Physical Response-Female was in order now that Jamie was a candidate. She was afraid that his kisses would distort the average. Certainly no other man had even come close to affecting her so strongly.

She was a bit worried. It was possible that Jamie's performance in the Sexual Attraction categories would influence his other numbers as well. Already she was feeling rather benevolent about what she'd perceived as his faults. Two or three more dates, and who knew what would happen? She might get entirely carried away and do something rash. She might disregard her carefully plotted intentions and rework the numbers so that the Love Bytes program would choose Jamie Flynn as her ideal match.

Incredible. Impossible!

As a scientist, she was supposed to be objective. Then again, the whole point of Love Bytes was to organize and evaluate her opinions. To a degree, Kate reminded herself. Some of her categories were scored on a predetermined scale. For instance, a career as an engineer or professor earned more points than bartending. It was a matter of stability, salary and education—not subjective at all.

She had to remember that her purpose was to choose the man who best embodied the traits of a lifetime mate, not to surrender to the fleeting thrall of infatuation.

Which she was admittedly on the brink of doing.

Incredible. But, however much her practical mind denied it, it was very, very possible!

Kate struggled to contain what she'd always viewed as her more unreliable emotions. This was one time a cool head *must* prevail. A risk-free marriage and secure future were at stake.

Taking a deep breath, she followed Jamie into the rustic kitchen of the modern farmhouse. A blackened hulk of a wood stove dominated the large room, which glowed with the homey warmth of satiny, hand-rubbed, handmade furnishings and cabinets. Windows of assorted sizes and shapes were flooded with sunlight, curtained only by the flowers and foliage of hanging baskets. Charity Castle stood at a flour-dusted chopping block, pummeling a lump of bread dough.

Charity was fifty-something, a short dumpling of a woman with frizzy, silver-tipped dishwater blond hair. Her grandmotherly appearance misled acquaintances into assuming she was a sweet-tempered earth mother. In Charity's case, though, the soft curves and nurturing manner camouflaged a spine of steel and the attitude of a drill sergeant. Her eyes were a soft suede blue behind her granny glasses, but her tongue was sharp. Kate had seen Charity turn a snotty, disobedient adolescent into a compliant pudding with no more than a few choice words.

And Charity was Jamie's mother-in-law? They made an odd combination. She'd keep an eye on the situation. It was bound to be interesting seeing how Charity handled Jamie. And vice versa.

When Charity saw their huckleberry harvest she clapped her floury hands and said, "Well done, people. Now you may clean them."

"Give us a break," Jamie groaned. "We're all wrung out from the picking." He slapped Charity's round rump on his way to the old-fashioned larder, where he emptied one of the buckets into a bowl.

"I can see that, Jamie." Charity's eyes swiveled from one to the other, making Kate very aware of her damp shirt and flushed face. "Terribly hot, isn't it, Kate? A shame you and the dear boy had to get so worked up."

Cleaning berries was preferable to answering such pointed questions. Remembering why Charity was always put in charge of their school's annual Christmas program, Kate silently tied back her hair with the red bandanna and settled at the kitchen table.

"Miss Suzannah will help. If you can find her." Charity dropped the bread dough into a mixing bowl and covered it with a linen cloth. She set the bowl on the broad sunny sill of a Palladian window. "I sent that girl out with the wash and haven't seen her since."

"I'll go and look for her," Jamie volunteered cheerfully, pausing to snitch some of Kate's cleaned berries on the way out.

Charity reached across the table and slapped his hand. "Hands to yourself, boy. Do try to obey—this time." Jamie's response, a lazily defiant laugh, carried over the wheeze of the swinging screen door as he exited. Charity pursed her lips at Kate.

Kate ducked her chin and pretended deep concentration on fishing leaves from the huckleberries. She was never quite sure how to take her fellow schoolteacher. And Jamie being Charity's son-in-law only complicated the matter.

"He's a rapscallion," Charity said with an affectionate *tsk-tsk*.

"Yes."

"But lovable, just the same."

Yes. Kate suppressed her instinctive response and instead said rather carefully, "I find I enjoy his company."

"How was it you persuaded him to chaperon your field trip?" Charity asked. "Even I have not been able to convince Jamie to get involved in that type of thing. Not since he wound up selling Girl Scout cookies out of the bar because Suzannah had come down with chicken pox." She clucked, shaking her head. "Jamie refused to go door-to-door."

Kate dropped a handful of berries into the colander. "I simply went to Huckleberries and asked him to volunteer. He was reluctant, at first."

"I wonder what changed his mind."

Do you really? Kate thought, wondering about how Charity felt, seeing her late daughter's husband with another woman.

"Has he told you about Sunny?" Charity asked abruptly.

Kate shook her head. "Sunny was your daughter?" she murmured, absentmindedly pinching a huckleberry between her forefinger and thumb until it burst.

Charity nodded. "My Sunshine."

Kate wiped her fingers on her pants. "Do you mean...as in Sunshine Castle?"

"A ridiculous name, in retrospect, but Sunny liked it well enough to give it to Suzannah as a middle name. It was appropriate for its time, and fortunately it fit Sunny well. She was our golden love child." Charity nodded toward an ancient round-shouldered refrigerator. A gallery of photos were stuck to it in magnetized frames. Many featured a short, curvy blonde as she aged from childhood to early motherhood—but not beyond.

Jamie's wife, Kate thought, disturbed that she should feel a twinge of envy toward the woman. Sunny was not outright beautiful, but her looks were enhanced by a spirit lively and strong enough to be captured on film. She seemed heartbreakingly young. And Jamie—in one of the photos he was a skinny young man not much older than twenty, with hair so short it looked military, holding a redheaded baby in one arm, the other around his smiling wife. Tears welled in Kate's eyes. She seemed to be readily susceptible to sentimentalism these days.

She swallowed. "How did she . . ."

"Leukemia," Charity supplied. "She was twenty-three. Suzannah was only five."

"How terrible."

"It's been almost ten years now, and life does go on," Charity said with the kind of equanimity only time and distance can bring. With a flick of her thumb, she pushed her wire-framed glasses up the bridge of her nose. "We've all learned that firsthand."

"You and Whistler are still close to Jamie."

"He's our son." Matter-of-fact.

"He had a rough childhood?" Kate probed.

Charity grabbed the colander. "If you've been to Huckleberries, you've met his mother, so make your own educated guess," she said, briskly rinsing the berries under the tap.

"No, I'm certain I haven't met her."

Charity stood on her toes to peer through the diamond-shaped window above the sink. "Where are those two? I swear, that Jamie is as big a goof-off as his daughter. Lazy as the day is long, the both of them!"

Charity was an excellent judge of character, and Kate knew she should take note of the older woman's assessment of Jamie even if it didn't bode well for his Love Bytes score. Worriedly Kate bit her lip; she was no longer so eager to find fault with him.

Charity drained the colander and returned it, empty, to the table. "Whistler will make us a pie when he returns from town. And Jamie can crank the ice-cream maker." She swept the kitchen with her gaze before settling across from Kate, satisfied that everything was under control. "I believe in keeping men busy. Otherwise, the rascals tend to get us ladies into trouble."

Laughter erupted from Kate's mouth before she could stop it. "Nicely put."

Sunlight reflected off Charity's glasses as she chuckled and nodded. "You will be careful around our dear Jamie, then? He's the worst."

Kate hesitated, then asked, "Do you mind me being here?" She had intended to say "being with Jamie," but was leery of the connotation. She couldn't explain about Love Bytes. As a sensible sort, Charity might understand its potential for the woman of the nineties, but then again, she might also feel it necessary to warn Jamie of Kate's secret motives.

Charity reached across the refectory table and squeezed Kate's hand. Guilty about accepting hospitality under somewhat false pretenses, Kate answered the overture with a tremulous smile.

"We're all glad Jamie brought you for a visit. I'd've introduced you two years ago if I'd had any inkling that he'd be interested in—" Charity angled her head apologetically "—your type."

"I know what you mean." Glumly, Kate's mouth turned down at the corners. "The thought of me and Jamie? Together?" She waved her blue-stained fingers. "That's absurd."

"Not necessarily absurd. Only surprising."

"You can say that again."

Charity rolled a stray huckleberry from hand to hand, a gesture Kate noticed in particular because it was so unlike Charity to fidget. "I do hate to interfere," she said with reluctance.

Kate nodded.

"But since you're not the typical sort of woman Jamie sees—even though he doesn't bring them here, word gets around, you understand—well, I should warn you. The fact is that Jamie is not a marrying man. Don't count on him for the long run, Kate."

Kate felt heat rising up her throat, flooding her face. Was her mission so obvious? Did she come across as such a desperately lonely old maid that even Charity had felt compelled to warn her off?

"He and Sunny married very young. Our little Suzannah Sunshine was on the way. We have no way of knowing if the marriage would've lasted, of course, but they seemed very happy, very devoted, and—"

"Of course no one can take Sunny's place," Kate said in a low voice. She closed her eyes.

"Not necessarily, Kate," Charity said, dubious but kind. "As I said, it's been almost ten years. It may be Jamie is finally dating a woman of substance because he's ready to try marriage again."

Kate shook her head with vehemence, her eyes still screwed shut. "No, please, you don't have to say that, Charity. We're not that serious about each other, anyway. I'm seeing other guys." Images of Love Bytes files danced on her inner eyelids. "I know Jamie is not the man for me." She blinked rapidly.

Charity looked ruminative, but she shook her head. "I've said my piece. I'm going to stay out of this from here on out. I despise busybodies."

Kate's eyes were bleak. "But I am glad Jamie brought me here, so you and I could get to know each other outside of school...." She went on for a time, blathering without listening to her own platitudes. Inside, she was devastated. For no good reason, she lectured herself. She'd known all along that Jamie was not her perfect match. Including him in Love Bytes had been an amusement. A momentary whim. She'd been no more serious about Jamie than he was about her.

Very convenient for both of them.

Kate dumped a slightly mushy clump of huckleberries into the colander. Charity had busied herself at the sink. *Thank you, Mrs. Castle,* a voice in Kate's mind chorused like a chastened schoolgirl. *Consider me warned.*

Whistler arrived with a bag of groceries. He hailed Kate heartily and grabbed Charity to blow raspberries on her plump cheek. Suzannah and Jamie burst into the kitchen with a slam of the screen door. They were both wet from dripping red heads to squidging sneakered toes. Jamie's blue jean cutoffs clung to him impressively and he'd discarded his T-shirt again. Kate made herself turn her gaze away. Suzannah, tossing her bedraggled braid as she flounced across the kitchen, distracted Kate with a wary, measuring sidelong look. The kind of look a teenager gives a schoolteacher who has stepped out of her place.

"You've been lallygagging at the swimming hole," Charity accused. She pushed her granddaughter toward the back stairs. "Into dry clothes, Miss Suzannah. Now. As for you—" she rounded on Jamie, pointing at his bare chest "—into clothes of any sort! What will our guest think?"

"Maybe that she wishes I'd invited her to come along," Jamie said, with a sly wink at Kate. "Sorry, Kate. Going swimming was a spur-of-the-moment impulse. Suze dared me to do a double somersault cannonball off the highest branch of the old elm."

"Did not," Suzannah called as she clattered up the stairs. "You dared *me!*"

"Whichever." Eyeing the diminished huckleberries, Jamie sat beside Kate. "I should have come back sooner to rescue you from Grandma Charity, resident slave driver."

Kate couldn't look at him, but he was so big and bare and wet and male neither could she look elsewhere. "We've been talking," she muttered.

"Uh-oh. What horrible things did Char say about me?"

Charity snapped a dish towel at him. "Nothing but the truth—and if it hurts, so be it. I'll show you from slave driver, Mr. Huckleberry. Get dressed and get to work. Kate and I decided we want homemade ice cream with our pie. Whistler—"

Whistler immediately threw up his hands in surrender. "I know, I know. Piecrust." He flipped open the cabinet that contained the flour bin. "You love me for my piecrust."

"No, I love you for your zucchini bread," said Charity, dropping a butcher-style apron over his balding, ponytailed head. "I'd marry you for your piecrust."

"Hey, Whistler, did I just hear a proposal? Finally?" Jamie said. "It must be the apron that got her. You look mighty fine in an apron."

Whistler threw a black glare over his shoulder. "And you do your best to keep me in one, don'tcha, Huck?" He scooped flour from the bin. "If I wasn't at the age where indoor plumbing is more of a necessity than a luxury, I'd tell you to take your cooking job and shove—"

"It in your big, fat mouth," Charity interrupted, with a pat of Whistler's grizzled cheek. "Do keep it shut. I've become accustomed to hot water on tap." She glanced at Kate.

"We roughed it for more years than I care to remember, on principle. We were quite noble, but also penniless."

"Until they caved and got regular jobs like the rest of us," Jamie said.

"With the exception of you guys in management, who never lift a finger unless it's to exploit their workers," groused Whistler.

Kate, silently following the banter, likened it to attending a Ping-Pong match. These people were rather loud and cantankerous. Positively . . . rambunctious.

"Commie," Jamie said cheerfully.

Whistler let fly. "Capitalist pig."

"Boys!" warned Charity.

"I'm sick of huckleberries," Suzannah said, coming back into the kitchen wearing dry shorts and a neon pink crop top. She twined her arms around Charity. "Gran, can't we please have an apple pie for a change?" Soon the entire group was arguing about the dinner menu.

Kate watched thoughtfully. Each was a true individual, unconditionally accepted by the others. Belatedly she realized that they were actually the best, truest kind of family—legalities and blood ties to the contrary.

She felt very much the outsider. Again.

5

JAMIE COULDN'T FIGURE OUT what had gotten into Kate. He'd switched shifts with Manny Delgado to free up an evening, but when he'd asked her out she'd claimed to be busy grading summer school projects and papers. Then she'd slunk into Huckleberries around nine that night looking sheepish about being there. She'd proceeded to hang out with the regulars—Roger and Rex, Millie, Cecil, the Folger twins in their plumber's whites—for almost two hours.

Since he'd let Manny leave early, Jamie had been able to snatch only a minute here or there to visit with her. She'd drunk a couple of weak wine spritzers. Then, while Jamie seethed from his position behind the bar, she'd allowed Tim Folger to escort her out of Huckleberries. Once he'd been backed into the corner of a booth and threatened with a lapful of hot espresso, Tim, a loudmouth no-talent pitcher on the hardware store's softball team, had admitted he'd only walked Kate as far as her car. She hadn't even given him her phone number. Jamie had decided to let Tim live.

At the end of the week, Jamie reverted to the safety of the daytime outing in case that was what had scared Kate off. He asked her if she'd like to come to Team Huckleberries' Saturday softball game. She politely declined—no excuse. Jamie made three errors during the game. Worse, the Folger twins teamed up to strike him out. Not even the soothing attentions of Yvette, the softball groupie he'd found pleasing enough in the past, made up for that. Fickle Yvette had then turned to Tim Folger for consolation. Or maybe it was Tom.

Then, to make a bad thing worse, as Jamie had been leaving the park after the game he'd spotted Kate arm in arm with a tall, dark-haired man carrying a picnic basket. They were walking toward the band shell, looking very cool, calm and compatible. Jamie's blood had boiled.

He'd lain in bed the rest of the evening, remembering the strains of the classical music drifting over from the park until his thoughts were turbulent. Although he preferred Bachman Turner Overdrive to Bach, he would've listened to it for Kate's sake. He would've tried the goose innards pâté and fish eggs that the picnic basket had probably contained. He even would've discussed the amusing presumption of the wine. With a straight face.

For Kate.

He wanted her. He thought she wanted him. Yet . . .

If they had a chance to last, he would have to somehow become good enough for her, even though feeling that he wasn't in the first place made him uncomfortable and dissatisfied. But also inspired.

Which wasn't a bad thing, he decided. Perhaps he'd fallen into a rut, settled for less than he should. Meeting Kate had given him the jolt he needed to get his life back on track.

It had been entirely different with Sunny—no deep thinking or self-evaluation required. Back then he'd been young, randy and on leave from a stint in the marines. Sunny had been eighteen, his long-distance sweetheart; she'd been a wildly creative artist, impetuous and free. They'd made a baby in the front seat of Whistler's VW, which was no mean feat.

Sunny hadn't cared about getting married, but she'd wanted the baby. Being more aware of how illegitimacy could feel to a child, Jamie had insisted they make it legal.

He'd taken an honorable discharge and settled down in Belle
Terre, intent on providing a secure home for Suze. And the
marriage had been mostly good, even with Sunny's occasional whimsies, like the time she'd wanted to plop the baby
in a backpack and hitchhike to California to swim in the
Pacific Ocean. In that case, Jamie had convinced her that a
scenic tour around Lake Superior in a borrowed camper
would do just as well. They had learned to compromise.
They'd learned that keeping their love and family together
was awfully hard work.

Sunny's leukemia had been lurking for years, though, and
she was gone before their sixth anniversary. Her death
changed Jamie—robbed him of his fledgling hopes and am-
bitions. He'd dropped out of the nighttime college courses
he'd been taking and wallowed in grief for several horrible
months, finding his only solace in the easy escape of alco-
hol because looking into his daughter's face hurt too much.
Thank God Charity had descended like an avenging—or
guardian—angel and snapped him out of his funk before
he'd gone the way of his mother.

One fine sunny day Jamie had found himself on the edge
of a steep cliff in Big Sur, holding hands with six-year-old
Suze, looking out at the ocean. He'd taken a good hard look
at himself as well, and when they got back to Wisconsin he'd
put a downpayment on the bar where he'd been working
and renamed it Huckleberries. He'd refurbished the place
and moved into the apartment upstairs.

Over the years, with Whistler and Charity's help, he and
Suze had worked out a new kind of family. Maybe it wasn't
the Ozzie and Harriet nine-to-five, white-picket-fence life
he'd once planned to give his child, but Suze had thrived just
the same. She was a good girl, if a bit too wild and impetuous, like her mother, and sometimes prone to low
achievement and procrastination, like her dad.

All in all, Jamie had been proud of his daughter, himself, his life. He was satisfied.

Then came Kate. And a whole other world of possibilities.

SUZANNAH FLYNN couldn't figure out what had gotten into her dad. All her friends used to think he was so cool—for a father—because he let her talk on the phone as long as she liked, have wild and rowdy sleepovers any night he was working late, which was practically *every* night, and ordered in pizza without nagging if she forgot again that it was her turn to cook when the bar was closed. She got to choose her own clothes, too, even if her clothing allowance wasn't as gigantic as Tiffany Blatnik's. Life had been practically perfect.

Then her dad had gone to one of those embarrassing parent-teacher conferences. Ms. Mallory must have snitched, because all of a sudden he'd said Suze couldn't use the phone or watch *Legends of the Fall*, which she'd already seen twenty-three times because she was in love with Brad Pitt, until her homework was finished. Then, as if forcing her to attend summer school wasn't bad enough, he'd given her a stupid computer for her graduation from junior high instead of the music store gift certificate she'd really wanted. And just to be sure her life was totally ruined, he'd hired Gregory Gordon Hodge to teach her how to use the software and cruise the Internet. Gregory Gordon Hodge! The dweebiest of the eighth grade computer dweebs! The complete and total opposite of Brad Pitt!

Well, aside from Ms. Mallory—who actually thought the class might like to take a field trip to Crystal Falls, Michigan to see the world's largest fungus—summer school wasn't so bad. Bryan Porter was in the same class and he was almost as good-looking as Brad Pitt, with the same initials even! Suzannah got to sit by him any time she beat Kirsten Danielson to the desk. Luckily, Kirsten was slow and Suzannah was fast.

And the computer was okay, too. She'd already mastered how to log on to the Brad Pitt Fan Club bulletin board, and it was kind of cool to e-mail friends all across the country.

Her dad had even promised her a bonus for fall school clothes. All she had to do to earn it was get a good grade in Ms. Mallory's summer school class. Suzannah was a little worried about the final exam because a new B.P. movie had just come out on video and she'd gotten kind of distracted from studying. But she had a plan. A really wicked plan.

All she had to do was sweet-talk Gregory Gordon into helping her out. Which shouldn't be too tough since she was afraid that he already had a crush on her. She'd absolutely *die* if her friends found that out!

"GREGORY GORDON?" Suzannah said softly, her chin in her hands. Her elbows were propped near the keyboard Gregory Gordon was hunching over, trying to demonstrate how Windows worked. "Could you do me an itty-bitty favor?" she asked, throwing in a flirtatious flutter of her lashes. A girl had to practice on someone, didn't she?

"Sure, Suzannah," Gregory Gordon squeaked. Then he blushed.

"Like, you know how Ms. Mallory's summer school classes just had finals?" Suzannah was sure he did. Even though he was a major brain, Gregory Gordon spent as much time at the school as the summer school students.

He nodded eagerly. "Your last class is next Tuesday, 10:00 a.m."

What had he done, memorized her schedule? Suzannah made a gritted-teeth smile. "Ms. Mallory will be passing out final grades. My dad's gonna *kill* me if I don't pass. Then I'll never get to the Lake Okanogobee beach, and I was gonna wear my new white bikini...."

Behind his aviator glasses, Gregory Gordon's eyes bulged. "That would be too bad," he said in a strangled whisper.

"So then could you maybe give me a peek at Ms. Mallory's grades on the computer? So, like, I'll have advance warning?"

"That would be hacking."

Suzannah tossed her long red wavy hair, bouncing slightly in her chair. "Yeah. Hackers are so cool, don't you think? Could you get into the school's computer system?"

"Of course. But that's illegal."

"Please, Gregory Gordon? Pretty please?"

"Just to look?" he bargained. "I won't change your grade."

"Just to look," Suzannah agreed, her fingers crossed under her chin. She knew for a fact that Bryan Porter had done worse than she had on the last test; she'd seen the blank spaces and the strike outs on his paper from across the aisle. Imagine how grateful he'd be if she could show him how to make sure his grade was high enough to get him back on the football team!

"This'll be a snap," said Gregory Gordon with confidence. "They basically have no security."

Suzannah's eyes widened. Wow, for a second there, nerdy old G.G. had looked almost cute! Totally weird, but now that the monitor was all lit up with numbers and letters reflecting blue off his lenses, he'd snapped back into total computer dweebdom, where guys like Gregory Gordon Hodge belonged. Whew. Close call!

Suzannah got herself back together in time to watch closely as Gregory Gordon started working on the password that would grant them access to the school's computer system. And Ms. Mallory's files.

JAMIE HEARD their voices, indistinguishable over the sound of the printer, as he opened the door onto the stairwell that led from the Huckleberries' kitchen to the four-room apartment above. He smiled. Despite Suze's initial protests, her lessons were progressing satisfactorily. Jamie was even thinking of having Gregory Gordon computerize the Huckleberries' business accounts.

The printer stopped. "What is it?" Suzannah said over the sound of crinkling paper.

"Statistics." Gregory Gordon sounded worried. "I thought these numbered subjects referred to students or classes, but now I don't know. This might not be about summer school at all."

"Well, I just want my grades. Where are they?"

"I must have gone into the wrong file by mistake."

As he came up the stairway Jamie had heard enough of their conversation to pique his interest. "Hey, kids," he said, entering the simply furnished living room where the computer sat on a desk in one corner. "What are you up to?"

Suze glanced up from stuffing a thick wad of paper into the wastebasket and he recognized her look of guilt. "Nothing, Dad. Just playing around." She kicked the basket under the desk as she rose. Her partner in crime shut down the computer.

"I thought I heard something about grades."

Suze shot Gregory Gordon a pleading look. He hesitated only briefly. "Upgrades," he explained, his downy cheeks reddening. "We were talking about upgrading your system, Mr. Flynn."

"So soon?"

Gregory Gordon's eyes shifted. "Y-you could maybe use another, uh, like, megabyte of RAM memory."

"Isn't the hour for my lesson up by now?" Suze interjected quickly. "Can I pretty please go to the beach, Dad? My friends have been there all morning. They've got killer tans."

Jamie checked his watch and nodded consent. She raced out of the room. "You've run over an hour, in fact," he said. The bedroom door slammed.

"You don't need to pay me overtime, Mr. Flynn, sir," Gregory Gordon said inching toward the door. "I have to go home now."

"Wait a minute. I owe you for the lesson."

"Pay me later." He bolted through the doorway and galloped down the stairs.

"So long, Gregory Gordon," Jamie murmured. His gaze went to the computer paper spilling from the wastebasket.

Suze flashed past, loose red curls streaming down the back of her white net beach cover-up. "See ya, Dad!"

"Be home for dinner," he yelled after her.

They usually ate downstairs in Huckleberries. Whistler was a stickler about Suze getting enough vegetables, and he refused to count the tomato sauce on a pizza.

After a brief debate on whether he was invading his daughter's privacy by doing so, Jamie pulled the clump of wrinkled computer paper from the wastebasket to have a look. Gregory Gordon had said something about statistics. These were statistics with a vengeance. Deciding the printout was innocent after all, and definitely indecipherable, Jamie started to shove it back into the basket. Then a name at the top of the first page caught his eye.

He read, *Project: Love Bytes. Katrina Mallory.*

Hmm.

Below that header was Subject #1KY in bold type, and then two columns of letters and numbers. Pers-62, Car-83, Et-45, Phys Att-20, and on and on. None of it made sense to him. Perhaps Kate was involved in some sort of science project and the kids had run across it by mistake. Which sounded likely... But a science project called *Love* Bytes?

He sat at the desk to skim down the list, smoothing the paper as he went. Subject #36TF was last on the list—skimpy data on that one, followed by several pages of complicated charts and what appeared to be mathematical equations. Then #1KY appeared again. Only this time around the information was more illuminating.

> Subject: #1KY
> Status: Divorced Once, Age 31
> Dependents: None
> Occupation: Medical Librarian
> Education: Masters in Library Science, UW-Madison
> Physical Description: 5'9", Brown/Brown, Approx. 145 lbs.,
> Bad to the Bone Tattoo (Right Bicep), Pierced Ear (Left)
> Dates Completed: Four
> Current Rank: 19th out of 36

Okay, the description established that #1KY was a man, not a fungus or a frog in formaldehyde. Possibly the subject was a woman, but the Dates Completed eliminated that possibility, even if the tattoo didn't. Providing that Katrina Mallory was the other half of the dating couple in question, of course.

Jamie suspected that she was. And he didn't like that one bit.

He flipped back to the earlier numbers. #1KY got a sixty-two in whatever Pers meant. Personnel? Personality? Persistence? A low twenty in Phys Att, but he must have a hot Car because it had earned him an eighty-three.

Love... Bytes, Jamie mulled. The words were an oxy-whatever, they didn't go together. What the hell was Kate up to? And how had his daughter and her computer tutor managed to get this printout?

Whatever it was, it was personal. He should throw it away and then read the riot act to Suze and Gregory Gordon about their unscrupulous hacking.

He knew he really should.

And he would.

The descriptions of Kate's subjects fluttered by as Jamie slowly smoothed and folded the long printout. #9BE was a forty-six-year-old cardiologist, #15OP a divorced electrician with four kids. Poor #23RP ranked dead last out of thirty-six. And #27CC...

He stopped to run his index finger down #27CC's data. The six-foot-three, brown-eyed and black-haired physical description matched up exactly with Kate's mystery date in the park. Apparently #27CC was a single, tenured professor with enough degrees to choke a bartender, whereas Jamie didn't have so much as a certificate in mixology.

#27CC had also completed *twelve* dates.

And he'd ranked Numero Uno.

But that was only a current ranking, Jamie thought grimly. It was beginning to be obvious that Love Bytes was a high-tech little black book. Only an uptight stick like Kate Mallory, otherwise known as Ms. White Wine Spritzer, could be so cool and calculating and judgmental as to categorize the men in her life like dead butterflies. And then rank her favorites.

Jamie thumbed through the printout until #34GH came up. A divorced mechanical engineer with a son named Gregory Gordon. The brush cut, the glasses. #34GH was Gordon Hodge. He was also Kate's current runner-up, although with only two dates completed there was an asterisk denoting that #34GH's data was incomplete. How open-minded of her.

Jamie turned over the last page of the printout. There he was—#35JF. He'd known it was coming, but seeing himself reduced to a few lines of print was more than dismaying. It was about as bad as coming upon your own obituary in the morning paper and having to pinch yourself to double-check your existence.

Or like trying to glimpse all of yourself in a mirror that was only an inch wide.

Suzannah was duly noted, and Jamie's hazel eyes and red hair. Kate had italicized the word *red*. She'd listed him as only a bartender, and put an asterisk after Education. Data incomplete. Two dates completed, another asterisk. A current rank of twenty-first out of thirty-seven.

Jamie's head snapped back. *Twenty*-freaking-*first?* Thanks a lot, Kate.

He pitched the printout across the room. It arced through the air, unfolding like an accordion and drifting to the carpet, a white ribbon of damning testimony on him and his pitiful existence.

No, he decided, slumping in the desk chair. The numbers damned Kate, not himself. Still…*twenty-one.* He was only number twenty-one.

So, okay. If that was the way that Kate wanted to play it, then that was how he'd proceed. There had to be ways to elevate his low ranking—even if he had to get down and dirty to do it. Even if he had to risk any remote chance he'd ever had that she might take him seriously. By the looks of his rank, that chance had been not much better than a million-to-one shot anyway.

After five minutes of heavy thought, Jamie picked up the end of the printout and began reeling in the scroll of incriminating statistics. First he had to decipher the mysterious notations, charts and equations.

Then, despite his rising sense of the absurdity of it all, he was going to devise a way to teach Kate Mallory the kind of lesson she'd never forget.

Because, Love Bytes or not, he still wanted her.

WELCOME was spelled out in twigs on Kate's front gate; Jamie wondered if the greeting would include him if Kate had any idea of his mood. On this particular humid summer afternoon, he was no jovial visitor. He was hot, inside and out. He was teetering on the edge, and he'd see to it that Kate soon joined him there. Then they'd go over the edge together...

Outward appearance belying his inner turmoil, Jamie strolled casually up the cobblestone path, a brown paper bag cradled in the crook of his left arm. Kate lived in a storybook house, a Tudor-influenced cottage with steep slanted roofs that were punctuated by two tiny curved eyebrow windows. There were cascading window boxes and half-timber eaves, tall diamond-pane windows curtained in lace. The front door was set in a soaring A-frame foyer, but Jamie went around to the side, where he found a screen door that opened onto the kitchen.

Kate was inside, moving between the stove, a cluttered countertop and a small round kitchen table. Her feet were bare, her legs long and lightly tanned beneath a pair of creased khaki shorts. A tight tank top showed off her generous curves. With the brown sections of her hair knotted up at the back of her head, she looked like a true redhead, of the strawberry blonde persuasion, for the first time. She was humming under her breath, preoccupied with her tasks.

Jamie smiled with dastardly intent. Kate had no idea what was in store for her.

When Kate caught sight of him lurking outside her kitchen door she almost dropped the glass jar she was holding with tongs. "You scared me," she gasped. "I didn't see you."

Jamie didn't move, or say a word. Kate swiped the back of her hand across her eyes, but the mesh of the screen door still blurred his silent, watchful figure. If it hadn't been for the billows of steam that had already fogged the room, Kate might have thought that the thick, hot, stifling miasma was rolling off of Jamie.

Carefully she set aside the hot jam jar, fresh from its boiling bath, then wiped her hands on the back of her shorts. Jamie nudged the door open with his toe. "Hi, there."

"Hi," she said with a breathy gulp.

"It's been a while." Jamie slumped against the door frame, his hands tucked into his pockets. "You've been busy."

His voice was almost a growl. Kate frowned, not sure of his meaning—especially as she'd been trying to avoid him. Rather unsuccessfully. "It's all those huckleberries Charity gave me," she said. "I've made huckleberry muffins, cake and bread. Now I'm canning the last of them."

"So that's why it's so steamy in here."

"Yes." The bubbling pots on the stove might have given him a clue.

"Don't get burned."

Kate's eyes narrowed as she retrieved a big wooden spoon, now dyed blue several inches up the handle, and started stirring. "It's the huckleberries that'll burn, not me."

"Mmm, maybe."

"Well, come on in, I guess," she said. It wasn't so bad, having him show up on her doorstep unannounced. That way she could see him and not take responsibility for initiating the contact. Also, there was Love Bytes to think about. Jamie's statistics were as yet incomplete. "What's in the bag?"

"The makings for strawberry margaritas."

Kate's mouth dropped open. The spoon hung in the air, dripping sticky syrupy jam on the floor until Jamie took it from her limp hand and laid it aside. He slipped past her, brushing so lightly against her backside she should have been scarcely able to feel it. But she did. So much so she thought her head was going to have to blow steam like a pressure cooker on high heat.

"You forgot," she said. "I don't drink margaritas."

"I didn't forget." Jamie touched the back of her neck with a fleeting caress. "It's time you did. Drink them," he added with a deliberate purr. Kate held her breath expectantly, but he only dumped the bag on the countertop and wandered into her dining room. A few seconds later, piano music poured through the house. Debussy's *La Mer*, surprisingly enough.

She wanted to follow Jamie and ask how he knew Debussy, but the jam would scorch. "I didn't know you could play the piano," she called over the music, taking up the spoon again.

"Uh-hmm." His fingers rippled up the ivories. "There's lots of things you don't know about me."

"I'm beginning to realize that," she muttered.

Jamie raised his voice. "I can give you a list."

All of her Love Bytes victims should be so cooperative.

"It's more fun not to, though," he continued, abruptly switching to something rollicking and lighthearted she didn't recognize. Honky-tonk music.

Kate shuffled her feet. The floor was gritty with spilled sugar. Her fingers were sticky; perspiration was dribbling down her face and neck. The jam-to-be was a scalding, bubbling purple morass and she had all these jars to fill. . . .

Responsibility warred with indulgence. Licking her lips, she could almost taste its honeyed temptation.

Or was that a dozen jam pots calling her name?

Kate called the huckleberry broth ready and started filling jars to the accompaniment of Jamie's music. The old piano was horribly out of tune, but Jamie had the touch. *Ooh, bad phrasing, teach,* she scolded herself, even as fantasy took flight.

Sweet heaven, but she wanted him to touch her. Almost as much as she wanted to touch him. She wanted to run her palms up and down his body, stroke his skin, kiss the warm, concave nook between his shoulder and chest. . . .

Her hands shook. Purple dots stained the clean white dish towel she'd laid across the table.

Love Bytes didn't matter. Practicality and Character scores meant nothing. Kate stopped pouring with still an inch of liquid jam in the bottom of the pot. She was looking inward and realizing that, yes, it was true. Brain-o-matic Mallory had fallen head over heels into the gooey, sticky morass of infatuation, and now that she was stuck she finally understood its allure.

Pulse accelerating, Kate set the blue enamel cooking pot back on the stove. Jamie's music beckoned to her. She could no longer resist.

The piano was in the dining room, set against one of the walls she'd papered with an intricate navy and ruby William Morris print. It was a monstrous instrument, big and blocky, with chunky spindle legs and lots of detailed carving. Kate only touched it to dust it.

"Interesting piano," Jamie said. He was playing "Camp-town Races."

"It came with the house." Kate slid onto the bench beside him. "I don't play. Where'd you learn?"

"Honky-tonk bar on the Mississippi," he sang, roughly fitting his words to the music. "Doo-dah. Doo-dah. An old guy there took me under his wing. Oh, the doo—"

"How old were you?" Kate interrupted.

"Maybe around ten, eleven, I forget. Before I discovered girls, anyway."

"You were hanging out in bars when you were ten or eleven," she said slowly.

"Uh-huh." He crashed all ten fingers on the keys, making the old piano reverberate with sound. "How about those margaritas?"

Kate followed him back to the kitchen. "I have to put the lids on my jam jars first."

Jamie did it, holding the hot jars with the dish towel, twisting the lids on tight with quick, sure movements that mesmerized Kate. She stared at his strong forearms, his capable hands until the word *ice* broke through her concentration.

"I need ice," Jamie said again. On the countertop, the contents of his paper bag were now interspersed among her utensils. Frozen strawberries, two liquor bottles, a lime. He opened the freezer compartment of her fridge and started pulling out trays. "Lots of ice. And a blender."

"I have a blender." As Jamie cracked the ice trays, sending the loosened cubes rattling into a ceramic bowl, Kate opened the cabinet where the blender was kept on a high shelf. She was reaching for it, her arms extended overhead, when a sharp, cold, shocking sensation at the small of her back froze her in midstretch.

6

KATE YELPED. Jamie pressed the ice cube hard against her skin, then slowly began to ease it up along her spine. She clung to the edge of the cabinet with her fingertips as she arched away from the cold caress. A shiver ran through her.

"Sorry," Jamie murmured. His laugh was low and rough-edged. "I just couldn't resist." His icy fingertips slipped beneath her stretchy lace tank top. Cold runnels of the melting cube trickled down to the small of her back, wetting the waistband of her shorts. Kate's body stiffened, then sagged.

"Mmm, that's...marvelous," she whispered. "So cold." Her head hung between her straining arms. When Jamie nudged the cube higher along the bumps of her vertebrae she sucked in a shallow breath and twisted slightly. Her breasts felt heavy and full, the nipples engorged, tingling painfully against the scratchy, abrasive lace molding them.

Jamie stood behind her, his thighs pressed to the back of hers. He put his left hand low on her stomach, providing a buffer between her hipbones and the biting edge of the countertop. The ice cube, now cupped in his hand, was melting fast. He rubbed it between her shoulder blades with the heel of his palm.

Kate squirmed; her breasts and backside swayed seductively. Jamie's breath puffed hot at the back of her neck. "Don't do that again," he warned.

She lifted her head, a small smile curving her lips. "Do what?" Another shiver gripped her and she wiggled with it, her hips shimmying with an extra, intentional provocation. "That?"

"Yes, that," he panted. A hard bulge nudged between the separation of her buttocks. Kate's chuckle was soft and insinuating. Apparently Jamie brought out the seductress she hadn't realized was hiding inside her schoolmarm exterior. Lucky him. *Lucky her.*

"I couldn't resist," she purred.

The cube had melted down to a smooth, icy shard. Suddenly Jamie pulled away, yanking her shorts out with one hand and slipping the other past the gaping waistband. His bunched knuckles stretched the elastic of her underpants, allowing his fingers to find the cleft of her derriere.

Kate gasped as he dropped the ice and withdrew. It slithered inside her panties, shockingly cold. She hopped in place, doing an impromptu, barefooted jitterbug on the grainy linoleum as the shard slid lower, tingling and teasing her hot flesh as it swiftly melted away to nothing.

Mortified, her chin came up as she swung around to accuse him. "Jamie!"

"I couldn't resist," he taunted.

Silent laughter trembled her lower lip. She put her hands flat against her flushed cheeks as if the gesture could contain the arousal fluttering through her. Pure, spine-tingling, uninhibited arousal—such a rush she didn't want to stop it even if she could.

Jamie advanced again. With his hands around her waist, he hoisted her up to sit on the kitchen counter among the bottles and measuring cups. A few of the items might have toppled; Kate wasn't paying attention.

She placed her hands on his face in turn, her fingertips moving wonderingly as they caressed his wide, ruddy-skinned cheekbones. He turned his head and kissed her palm, then, eyes sparking, gently bit the mound below her thumb. His tongue licked the jammy stickiness from her palm, slipped lower to soothe the thready pulse beat at her wrist. "So frantic," he murmured. "Don't be afraid, teach. Just tell me what you want."

What *did* she want? The answer was simple—she wanted to surrender to impulse, however shocking. And she wanted Jamie.

She leaned back. The ceramic bowl filled with ice was within reach. "I want you to take off your shirt."

"Yes, ma'am." Jamie's mouth curled into a tight smile. After he'd peeled off his striped rugby shirt and tossed it aside, he wore only bleached jeans, riding an inch below his navel, stretched taut across the fly. Kate thought he was more than handsome—he was utterly, desirously masculine.

With delicate precision, she selected a cube. "Now I want you to come here."

He cocked his head, evaluating her position with a leisurely, brooding perusal. "First you'll have to open your legs."

Kate's eyes widened. She stared down at her bare thighs, clamped together, her tightly crossed ankles. The ice was dripping in her hand, a clock ticking loudly on the wall. Much as she wanted to, she couldn't make herself comply.

Jamie took another ice cube and slowly, precisely eased it along both of her legs, laying slick cold trails along the quivering muscles of her thighs, down her shins to her twined ankles. "Relax," he coaxed, lowering his head so he could lick at the wetness. His palms were warm, sliding over her skin, slipping in between her knees and dipping lower, smoothly unlinking her ankles. "Relax." Kate exhaled a huge, shaky breath and let her legs dangle.

Jamie put his hands under the backs of her knees and parted her thighs as he stepped between them. He scooted her bottom across the counter so she was snugged up against him, her partially bared abdomen melding to his hot bronzed skin. The kitchen windowpanes were fogged with steam, trickling with moisture; humid ninety-eight degree air curled past the screens.

Jamie's eyes were narrow and eerily incandescent. Kate's heart raced in response. "We won't do anything you don't want to do," he promised, but his voice bore a trace of menace and she wasn't particularly comforted. She was, however, feeling reckless enough not to care.

Licking salty perspiration from her upper lip, she un-fisted her hand and held out the half-melted, malformed ice cube, her palm gleaming wetly. "Is this—" Her voice shook with nervousness. She swallowed and tried again. "Is this what you want?"

"For starters," answered Jamie with a small smile.

She pouted her lips, hesitated, then made a quick gesture toward his jeans. He tried to back away, but she'd hooked her finger in his waistband. The snap popped. She pretended to peek inside, dangling the ice cube between two fingers.

"I wouldn't," he admonished.

She palmed the cube. "No, I suppose not. We don't want you to, um, *melt* so soon." Instead she took an ice cube in both hands and brushed them over his forehead, down his temples, across his cheeks. Playfully she inserted one between his lips and he sucked at it, catching the drippings on his extended tongue. She took the cube back with her own mouth, her lips gliding cold across his, making his head thrust forward aggressively to steal another taste.

"No, no, no," she breathed, putting one wet, numb hand across his mouth as her head dipped to his shoulder. She worked the ice cube in and out of her mouth as she lathed his perspiring skin, creating a provocative, contrasting play of alternately warm and cold lips and tongue, the intermittent shock of frigid ice. Finally the cube was no more than a sliver and she tilted her head way back, letting it slide down her throat.

Jamie groaned. "My turn."

"Not yet." Indiscriminately Kate plunged her hand into the bowl. Frosty cubes skated across the countertop. "I haven't finished."

"Well, try to finish before I do," he said tightly.

"Let's try...this." With no more warning, she touched two ice cubes to his chest, smiling in satisfaction as he flinched, his nipples tightening into small brown beads that she flicked with her icy fingertips because using only the hard frozen cubes would deny her the tactile pleasure.

"Enough already," Jamie said, and lunged to capture her mouth. Her tongue was cold, but it warmed up in only seconds as he kissed her lavishly, hungrily. Kate surrendered with a soft moan, dropping the ice cubes so she could clutch at his broad back as he bent over her, driving her backward into the cabinet with the force of his passion. Molten desire poured through her, melting her bones, liquefying her insides, flooding her erogenous zones until she felt full and swollen and crazy for even more.

Crazy, she had to be crazy! She *couldn't*— But the inner protest was fleeting. She was beyond caring.

Without relinquishing her mouth, Jamie peeled the lace top up over the creamy curves her unbound breasts. He rolled her nipples beneath his thumbs, cupping her breasts in his large hands, his fingers kneading the opulent flesh until she was quaking with pleasure.

Quickly ducking past the tangled strip of her tank top as she pushed it over her bent head, Jamie unerringly homed in on one of her thrusting nipples, taking it deep into his mouth. She cried out, feeling the tugging of his lips all the way to her womb. With blind fingers he found a slivered shard of ice and popped it into his mouth as he switched his attentions to the other stiff pink nub, then back up to her lips. Their icy-hot kisses were sumptuous and salacious.

Jamie kicked off his shoes, unzipped and shoved his jeans and boxer shorts down until they dropped to his ankles. Kate was trembling violently, her eyes bright emerald, wide-open in sharp awareness as she lifted her hips so he could slide away her own remaining garments.

"Is this what you want?" he rasped, touching her intimately. His face was drawn, his eyes fierce. His fingers speared through her yielding flesh. "This?"

"Yes." She ran shaky fingers down his chest, over his flat stomach. After a split second of hesitation, she took his erection in both hands. It was impossibly rigid. She stroked the swollen length of it, drawing it toward the patch of red-gold curls between her widespread thighs. But when he was poised to enter, his hands on the backs of her legs, levering them up, she looked over his shoulder and gasped, "The door!"

He plunged inside her body, gliding deep in one smooth stroke, eliciting an involuntary high-pitched whimper. "The—door," Kate panted, twining her legs around his waist so he was clasped to her. "Someone—might—look in."

"Should I leave you?"

Her slick satin sheath tightened, preventing his withdrawal. "No." She was insensate.

Jamie still had the presence of mind to step out of his discarded jeans. "Then I'll take you with me," he said, his fingers sinking into the bare flesh of her buttocks as he lifted her from the kitchen counter.

"You can't possibly—" Her protest died as he did exactly as he'd said. She clung to him like a barnacle for the five-step journey to the open door. Frantically she swiped at it, swinging it away from the wall, just missing clipping her out-thrust backside by an inch. Jamie lurched forward, slamming the door shut as their combined weight collapsed against it.

Kate was pinned, naked and writhing. She'd never felt so exposed, so defenseless. Jamie's powerful muscles bunched under her hands as he drove up into her, his thigh propped beneath her for support.

They were both feverish with lust, sliding against each other, their bare skin slick with perspiration. For Kate the sensation was incredible, impossible, almost unbearable. Even though her head was spinning from the shock of it, unthinking primal abandon had for once taken control.

A shattering climax ripped through her. Coming without warning, it was tumultuous and convulsive, making her scream out the keening pleasure of it until Jamie captured her mouth with his to quiet her, gently easing her back to reality as the tremors gradually lessened, leaving her limp, languid, weak . . . and thoroughly, contentedly satisfied.

Jamie held her close. She whimpered softly and he kissed her pearly pink cheek. She cradled his head in her hands, her own lolling back as if her neck could no longer support it. Her body shifted imperceptibly.

"Oh!" In the still aftermath, the one word was a quiet bubble-burst of surprise. Kate shifted again, touching the toes of one foot to the floor. Jamie raised his head and looked her straight in the eye. She blinked.

He was still hard, lodged deep inside her. Another aftershock, a last, languorous shiver, rippled over her skin. Loosened reddish-apricot-brown hair fanned across the door, she sank a half-inch lower, taking him even deeper. Her eyes were huge, startled.

Jamie slid his hands down, under her thighs. Although he'd been ferocious in the initial coupling, almost furious, he was now taken with another mood entirely.

Kate had revealed herself. She was not the bloodless, coldhearted calculator of Love Bytes. Having felt her body give under his, having seen the soft sheen of emotion in her eyes, he could not maintain his cynicism.

He wanted to make love to her. Hot, sweaty, sweet, slow, any way at all, but definitely *making love*.

Without motive.

Kate closed her eyes and arched her back, tightening around him. "J-Jamie?" she whispered. One eyelid twitched.

"Hold on, Katy." He sensed that she was withdrawing mentally, so he took her mouth with his and kissed her for long, languid minutes, eventually beginning an unhurried, sensual rocking motion of his hips against hers. The door creaked. There was a look of astonishment of Kate's face.

She murmured with pleasure, then turned her head to one side, ducking her chin as if in embarrassment. Jamie trailed kisses across her shoulders and upper chest, admiring the rosy glow that matched the color in her cheeks, loving her sweet shyness, such a contrast to the abandon of moments before. He found her lips again and sucked and licked at them tenderly until she was smiling.

He stiffened, the muscles in his thighs quivering with tension. Kate squeezed her legs around his waist, putting her hands down to his flexing buttocks as he made one last deep thrust and groaned raggedly, finding fulfillment in a flash of white-hot pulsing pleasure.

ONCE AGAIN, Kate's emotions were all shook up. Her thoughts were fractured. On one hand, she felt blissfully content, her eyelids heavy as she lounged on her tapestry settee among soft, cloudlike piles of cushions beneath the *whump-whump-whump* of the ceiling fan, listening to a romantic recording of Liszt spilling from the CD player. Her skin was dewy and fresh from a cool shower, but still shimmering with pleasurable sensations.

On the other hand, *there was a near-naked man in her kitchen!* The blender whirred. *And he was making strawberry margaritas!*

Well, the situation could be worse. Jamie could be totally naked. He had been, in fact, standing quite unabashed before her refrigerator as he took out more ice. She'd insisted he at least put on his boxer shorts. They were conveniently nearby, after all—on the kitchen floor with the rest of their clothing—and they were patterned with tiny winged pigs. A fact she'd missed when he'd slipped out of them or she might've had second thoughts, she'd teased.

But seriously, the status of her Love Bytes project was more worrying than Jamie's state of undress. How was she to reconcile this interlude, in the kitchen of all places, with the Love Bytes ratings scales? Even with the equations that leveled the playing field, so to speak, Jamie's Sexual Attraction scores were sure to shoot him up the rankings. Probably from his current twenty-first position to single-digit territory. Maybe even the top five.

No, not that high, she assured herself, even as a part of her ached to rank him Number One. Had it been the heat of the moment, she certainly would have.

Fortunately, the entire intention of Love Bytes was to do away with the influence of the heat of the moment. No one could make a rational decision at such a time. Kate, herself, hadn't been capable of making a decision of any kind.

She punched a mop-fringed pillow and stuck it under her head. Was it any wonder so many marriages failed when the initial partnering was made under infatuation's heady influence?

Infatuation and lust, she thought. Their pull was stronger than she'd realized, but now she knew, oh, boy, did she. Firsthand.

She stirred, turning over onto her side. Planted by Jamie, the lure was there, an irrevocable part of her, strong and pulsating as a second heart. But still only infatuation. She could resist. Eventually.

She would have to if she was serious about selecting herself a husband. However, exactly why she'd decided it was time to do so seemed hazy to her at the moment. . . .

She struggled to remember. Okay, one, she'd been tired of living alone. Just because Jamie was here for the moment didn't mean he'd stay. Two, she wanted children, a family. She'd get a ready-made one with Jamie, if it came to that, although not the kind she'd envisioned as ideal. And three, what was three? There had seemed to be a million good reasons for Love Bytes when she'd begun, but now her sense of urgency was dulled.

That wasn't good, Kate told herself. She shouldn't stray from her course, especially since it wasn't as though Jamie were offering her marriage, or even commitment. Charity had specifically warned her about that, and all that Kate knew of him suggested the same. Jamie might be sexually masterful, but he was still a wisecracking, play-the-field, take-no-prisoners kind of guy.

True, now and then, she'd sensed a certain indefinable longing in him that perhaps reminded her of . . . well, of herself. And at times his caustic self-denigration seemed to hint that he wanted something of Kate, some acknowledgement. Of what, she wasn't sure. Or why. He'd always covered up his moments of vulnerability with a ready, puckish quip. And distracted her with a kiss or two. Or three.

Or more. The thought, the recent memory, was delicious.

"Thinking good thoughts, Katy?" Jamie asked as he entered the living room.

Kate bit back an involuntary, infatuated smile. There was no need to let him know just how good. And, in a way, bad.

"Strawberry margaritas," he announced, dropping smoothly to the cushions and offering her a frosty glass. "For my sweet, wild strawberry margarita woman." He kissed her.

She pushed herself up to a sitting position to take the glass. It was filled with dark pink slush and garnished with a plump strawberry. "I still can't believe that was me," she confessed.

"I'm not too good of a man to say—" he rolled the strawberry on his tongue and swallowed "—I told you so."

"Mmm," Kate murmured, not committing herself to anything. Yes, Jamie had demonstrated that she was a passionate woman. Yet . . . couldn't he see that passion was not the sort of emotion you could build on for the future? It was unreliable. It rarely lasted.

Then again, there was a strong passion throbbing within her even as they spoke. She couldn't deny that, either.

Feeling like Eve with the apple, she sipped the strawberry margarita.

Jamie's eyebrows went up. "So?"

"Tasty." She swirled her tongue around the lip of the glass. "What's in it?"

"Frozen strawberries, fresh-squeezed lime, orange liqueur. Tequila."

Kate took another sip. "And ice."

"Yes, ice. But not as much as originally required. I ran short."

"Or we ran long."

"Yes, that, too." He laughed. "I'm amending your newest nickname to Just Add Water—or Ice."

She was rapidly developing a taste for strawberry margaritas, damn the consequences. "It's lovely. Delicious."

"Go easy, Katy. The tequila packs a punch, especially if you're not used to it."

Kate sat forward, her loose nightshirt skimming her body. She was nude beneath the semisheer white gauze and Jamie had taken note, she realized with a tiny squiggle of bashful pleasure. Having the power to seduce was new to her. Or at least it was new for her to take particular notice.

"We should talk," she said.

"Uh-huh." Jamie slid to a slump, resting his shoulders against the seat of the old-fashioned tapestry settee. He put his glass aside and began to lackadaisically page through one of her collection of aged Victorian albums of pressed flowers and ferns, squinting to decipher the faded ink of the spidery handwritten Latin identifications.

Suddenly Kate felt cold, and it wasn't because of the icy cocktail. "Is that all right with you?"

He opened another album. Butterflies. "It's to be expected."

Kate got up, stalked across the sisal rug and dropped with a soft thud into a long teak deck chair she'd fitted out with petit point cushions. Fuming, she folded her legs to her chest and demanded, "What is?"

Jamie shrugged. "Monday morning quarterbacking. You either want to rehash the performance—should I say rate it?—or you want to have the big commitment talk."

Kate's heart skipped a beat. The part about ratings—he couldn't know! His wording had to be coincidence, nothing more. "I don't understand," she said carefully. "What are you hinting at?"

"Hinting?" His expression and gestures were filled with tension. There was an antique microscope on her coffee table and he used it as another distraction, twirling the copper knob with jerky motions as he peered into the eyepiece. "I thought I was being blunt."

"Blunt enough," she said in a huff.

Finally Jamie sat back and looked straight at her, his arms crossed behind his head. She didn't particularly care for that, either. "Okay," he said. "Let's talk."

Kate tossed her head. "Well, don't worry. It's not like I expect you to—to marry me!"

Total silence. She winced inside.

"That's a load off my mind," Jamie said dryly. So dryly his voice almost cracked.

"I'm quite aware that suggesting a commitment would also be asking too much of you," she added in a softer tone.

He tilted his head back against the settee and stared up at the ceiling. "If that's how you see it . . ."

Kate was confused. Jamie sounded almost as if he *wanted* her to ask it of him. Could that be?

He sighed. "But you do want to be married, I take it."

"Well, yes. Eventually." Like in the next few months. "I've always wanted a family, and it seems I've put if off long enough." She hesitated. "I expect to choose a suitable husband one day . . . soon."

Jamie was staring at her again, with eyes so dark and serious they looked like burnished antique gold in the narrow shaft of afternoon sunlight escaping a crack in the curtains. "Any prospects?" he asked, trying for flippancy. He didn't quite make it.

"Prospects?" Once more, they were approaching Love Bytes territory. Kate felt uncomfortable, as if Jamie were goading her.

"You know what I mean. How many eager young studs have applied for the job?"

She responded with stony precision. "I believe this conversation is inappropriate."

"Begging me to make love to you on the kitchen counter might also be considered inappropriate."

Kate shot to her feet. "I did not!"

Jamie was standing before her in a flash, his hair in wild tufts and tangles all around his head. "You did. And I loved it." He gripped her upper arms. "Dammit if I don't love you, too."

Her anger gave way to shock. "What?" she squawked.

"Don't make me say it again."

Kate's shoulders sagged. "You . . ." She couldn't say it either. "How could you?"

"I don't know, Katy. I don't know." His voice was ragged. "Don't worry, though. I'll handle it. I won't upset your perfect little life any more than I already have."

Suddenly he thrust her away and stormed into the kitchen. By the time she'd staggered after him, stricken with dawning awe, he was dressed and ready to go. The leftover margarita mix, half a blender full, was melting into watery pink soup six inches away from the patch of countertop where her body had begged for his. She'd thought it was just infatuation, chemistry, sex, but . . .

Jamie *loved* her?

"Please, wait," she pleaded when he opened the door.

He hesitated. "There's nothing else to say, Kate."

"What happened to *Katy?*" she asked. Her hands were shaking and she clasped them together, tucking them under her chin, which was shaking, too. Her whole body was shaking.

Jamie didn't look back. "Call me when you've figured it out."

And then he was gone.

JAMIE WHIPPED INTO Huckleberries like a tornado. He'd really blown it big time. From what he'd so far been able to deduce about Kate's Love Bytes project, hearing that one of her "subjects" loved her was the last thing she wanted.

He hadn't intended to say it. He hadn't even figured it out for himself. Kate was probably horrified now that it had sunk in, and wondering frantically how she was going to explain that he ranked only twenty-first on her list of potential husbands.

Oh, yeah, he'd really blown it.

"Whoa, watch out for the boss, Millie," warned Manny as he passed the gray-haired older woman a tumbler filled with clear liquid.

"Good ol' Huck looks like he's been rode hard and put up wet." Millie lifted her drink, sipped and smacked her lips with obvious relish.

Jamie snatched the tumbler from her hand and flung its contents into the sink behind the bar. "What was it this time, Millie?" he snarled. "Vodka? Whiskey?" He turned on Manny, grabbing the bartender by the collar. "How many times have I told you not to serve her the hard stuff?"

Manny shoved him away. "Cool it, Huck. It was flavored water, the expensive designer kind, that's all."

Jamie slammed his hands down on the bar. "Jeez, I'm sorry, Manny. I'm just—just—" He was at a loss for words. Too bad that hadn't occurred fifteen minutes earlier, when Kate had pushed him over the edge with her talk of "suitable" husbands.

Manny slapped him on the shoulder as he passed. "Don't worry about it, Huck. I'll live."

"Well, I'm not sure I will," Millie wheedled. "I'm an old lady and this heat is getting to me. I happen to be dying of thirst!"

Jamie was filling another glass for her as Cecil Apthorpe came into the bar. "Toodles, dollink," he said to Millie. "My, you're looking spiffy today. Huck doesn't appear as chipper, however."

Millie patted the stool beside her. "Take a load off, Cecil, you charmer. Maybe you can cheer m'boy, here, up."

Cecil tapped the mahogany bar. "Two fingers of Scotch, barkeep. I'm flush today. The Apthorpe family retainer has finally seen fit to send my quarterly dividend winging across the Atlantic."

"Hip-hip-hooray," cheered Millie.

Jamie catered to the raucous, unconventional pair in a moody silence. Funny thing. Although he'd just had the best sex of his life, he wasn't in a celebratory mood.

KATE STOOD FROZEN in the center of her living room, contemplating her "perfect little life."

The room was dim, genteel, sumptuous with shabby chic. Faded cabbage roses papered the walls below dark wood cornices, and more mismatched florals were layered elsewhere in the draped tablecloths and patterned pillows. Before the dark walnut mantle of the fireplace, a Chinese needlepoint rug was piled on a mossy green carpet piled on the sisal mat. She'd carefully gathered cherished items around her: the Victorian flora and fauna albums, antique microscope, leather-bound books, her Irish linen napkins and Georgian silver tea service.

Suddenly it all seemed so fussy. She could imagine herself a little old lady puttering among her things, perhaps still plotting how one day soon she'd find a gentleman with a perfect score.

Was that what she wanted? Or did she dare to be Jamie's Katy, and grab the gusto while she could? But what, then, of her future? Her oh, so reliable husband and their family-to-be?

Jamie had a family. Not necessarily the ideal, but still one she'd come to appreciate. Could she settle for that? Could she fit in?

Then again, he hadn't exactly offered. Had he?

Kate, the woman with all the answers, suddenly had none.

"*Oh*, Ka-aate!" Monica called through the screen door. "Here's hoping you're decent, 'cause I'ma coming in!" It was a frequent joke, based on the fact that Kate was never indecent. Little did Monica know that this was one time . . .

Kate expected a shocked gasp when her friend's sharp gaze fell on the discarded clothing, the puddles of melted ice, the margarita mix. Then she remembered that Jamie had cleaned up everything but the margaritas. There was something to be said for having a near-naked man in your kitchen, especially one who was thoughtful enough to straighten up after he'd provided you with the hottest sex of your life.

Monica peeked into the living room. "Kate? Is that you?"

"Technically speaking, this is all a result of brain-induced chemicals," she said. "Natural amphetamines. Dopamine, norepinephrine, phenylethylamine. They produce feelings of euphoria, sleeplessness, hope, apprehension, lust."

Monica's stare was blatant. Too late, Kate remembered her see-through gauze nightshirt. "Doesn't look like Kate, but it sure does sound like her," murmured Monica.

"It's called infatuation and it begins to dissipate by the fourth year. Often sooner."

Monica clapped her hand to her mouth. "It's finally happened."

"What?" Kate said, shaking her head as if she'd been awakened from one very mesmerizing dream.

"Hip-hip-hooray! You're in love," Monica cheered.

7

"THE JUXTAPOSITION of styles was stilted, at best. Nor was there synergy in the palette, what with all those dreadful reds and purple-tinted blues, like overripe fruit. And that murky Giulio Fabriani! Strictly second-class. I once saw a topflight Fabriani in, where was it, the Prado, I believe, during my sabbatical abroad. Ah, now that was a work of art, Katrina, a true masterpiece. They should have read my treatise on the use of earth tones in Fabriani's *il penseroso* period before purchasing..."

Kate's eyelids drifted shut as Cotter continued to pontificate. He needed little encouragement, in fact he probably preferred none. Fortunately he'd chosen the right profession, Cravenleigh College's Professor Cotter Coleman lived to lecture.

Kate snuggled deeper into the plush car seat. She'd been known to launch into stilted scientific speeches herself now and then, but usually Monica was there to snap her out of it. There'd been no problem communicating with Jamie, either, come to think of it. They'd talked about a lot of things during their times together—movies, politics, sports, music, families—and while they hadn't agreed on much besides Harrison Ford, Susan B. Anthony, Brett Favre, Mozart and the Brady Bunch, he'd never seemed bored by her in the least. Nor she by him.

Her eyes blinked open. The velvet darkness of the rolling Wisconsin countryside was rushing past the car window; a ghostly image of her own face was superimposed upon the glass. Kate grimaced at herself.

Okay, so she'd rather be out with Jamie. Monica may have been exaggerating, saying Kate was in love with him, but Kate was honest enough to admit that something important was growing between them. If it was only infatuation, it had to be the worst case known to womankind.

She would have done more research on the subject if Jamie had called. Too bad he hadn't. Cotter had, though, and she'd bowed to her responsibilities to Love Bytes.

On the Love Bytes rating scale, Cotter's impressive education had earned him many points. Jamie, on the other hand, claimed to have barely graduated from high school. But Jamie wasn't dumb. Unfortunately, she—er, Love Bytes—had made no provision for native intelligence. And no provision for pompous blowhards, either. But that was being too hard on Cotter.

She'd liked him fine until she'd begun comparing him with Jamie. Cotter was tall, dark and handsome in an elegant, urbane way. He was brilliant, or so he claimed. Even his lecturing voice was not unpleasant, rather like the drone of honeybees....

Kate's eyes closed again, and soon she was in a meadow, the grass and wildflowers as high as her waist, the sunshine like hot, golden syrup as it poured over her bare skin. A man approached, his bonfire hair aflame in the sweet liquid sunshine....

Gravel crunched beneath the wheels as Cotter turned the car into a dimly lit parking lot. "Where are we?" asked Kate, blinking back to reality. She unsnapped her seat belt and sat forward, peering through the windshield at an unassuming cedar-sided building. Her heart dropped.

"Yes, I know the place looks like a hole in the wall, Katrina, but I thought we should give it a chance. Nothing ventured and all that." Cotter chuckled at his own humor. "A friend of mine says the ambience is not all that it should be, but they have a chef who can actually distinguish between leeks and onions. Uncommon knowledge in a burg like Belle Terre."

Kate was staring, aghast, at the blue neon sign in the window. Huckleberries.

Cotter opened her door. She sat rigidly. "No, Cotter. Perhaps another time."

He took her hand. "Come, Katrina. Consider it slumming. An adventure among the riffraff!"

She resisted. "No. I have a headache."

He tugged her from the car. "Food will cure that."

"Cotter, I said no."

He looped his arm around her waist and propelled her toward the double doors. Kate felt like Marie Antoinette on her way to the guillotine, but Cotter blithely ignored all her protests. His Etiquette score had just taken a turn for the worse, she decided grimly, as he put his hand at the small of her back and more or less shoved her into Huckleberries.

The joint was, in a word, jumping. Kate peeked around the rough wooden archway of the foyer. There was a slight chance she could blend into the crowd.

Cotter stepped forward and raised his hand imperiously. A waitress in a blue Huckleberries apron hesitated on her way to a booth with a tray of drinks. "We'll take a table for two," Cotter commanded.

The waitress, middle-aged and frazzled, ran a dubious eye down Cotter's expensive tailored suit and took in his Hermès tie. Huckleberries' was a blue-jeans-and-sneakers crowd. "Suit yourself. Seat yourself, too," she added, cackling as she hurried away.

Cotter looked annoyed. He grabbed Kate's hand and strode toward the seating area without delay. Kate scurried after him, trying to duck behind his back when they passed the bar, but daring one quick glimpse over his shoulder. Manny Delgado was schmoozing with the customers. Maybe she'd gotten lucky and Jamie was off for the night.

"A booth," Kate muttered into Cotter's ear, sliding into the first available one she saw, without waiting for his approval. The padded bench seats were tall and she sat with her back to the bar, slouching toward the corner so she wouldn't be seen. "Let's only have drinks, Cotter. This really isn't your kind of place."

Using his fingertips, he plucked out the menus that were tucked behind the napkin dispenser and condiment squeeze bottles. "Have you no sense of adventure, Katrina?" He flicked open the menu. "Ugh, deep-fried mozzarella sticks."

Kate's chin sunk into her chest as she held her menu up over her face. It was a stopgap measure, at best. She was sure to be spotted and what would happen then was anyone's guess. If Jamie showed up, he was the type to create a scene, or so she suspected. She pictured chairs and bottles smashed, Cotter being thrown the length of the bar and through the window as in the fight scene from every Western ever made. Being nonviolent, she had no reason to find the possibility slightly thrilling. But she did.

The same waitress arrived at the table. "What'll it be?"

Cotter's aquiline nose twitched. "Is the shrimp fresh?"

"Fresh as it can be, considering we're a thousand miles away from an ocean," was her jaunty reply. Her gaze landed on Kate. "I've seen you in here before, am I right? At the bar?"

Kate hunched her shoulders, mumbling, "Umm, maybe."

"Katrina? You've been here before?" Cotter dropped his menu. "Why didn't you say so?"

Kate made a noncommittal gesture with one hand. Might Cotter be jealous? That possibility also seemed to rouse her interest. Up to now, their dates had been so stately and dignified and essentially uneventful that she'd begun to wonder if Cotter found her at all attractive. If he'd even noticed that she was a woman.

"Smart, sneaky Katrina, ferreting out the in-spots before they're trendy," Cotter continued, nodding at her acumen. "Then you can recommend the menu, my dear. I don't want anything fried, so that eliminates half the offerings. Shall I try the gazpacho to start?"

Kate gritted her teeth and smiled through the long process that Cotter made of ordering. By the time she left the table, Carole, the waitress, was also gritting her teeth. But not smiling.

Millie arrived several long moments of impending doom later, waving her arms even though she carried a mug of beer. "Howdy, folks!" Cotter stiffened as droplets splashed the tabletop. Kate shrank deeper into the corner of the booth, a move Millie took as an invitation. She plunked her mug on the table and slid in.

"Umm, Millie, this is Professor Cotter Coleman," Kate said. Millie waggled her eyebrows. "Cotter, Mil—"

"Millicent Flynn," the older woman supplied with a grand air, offering her hand. "Howdja do?"

Cotter murmured something halfway polite, but ignored Millie's hand in favor of fastidiously blotting the table with a paper napkin.

Millie flipped her gray braid. "He's a handsome one, Kate. But chilly." She made a shiver. "Brrr."

Kate tried to hide her face behind a hand cupped over her forehead; there were too many people she recognized among the Huckleberries customers. Why had she ever succumbed to the unlikely urge to spend so much time here lately? She must have watched "Cheers" one time too many.

Millie drained her mug and slammed it down. "And here I was thinking you and Jamie were..." Her brows waggled again.

Cotter's eyes narrowed. "Were what?"

"Ridin' the rapids," she said. "Punchin' the hole in the doughnut."

"What is this woman talking about?" Cotter demanded. "And who is Jamie?"

"Cuttin' the hay. Shuckin' the corn." Millie hee-hawed like a mule. "Runnin' the old flag up the flagpole and givin' it the bare-butt salute. Haw! Haw! Haw!"

Kate dropped her face into her hands.

"Katrina?" Cotter sounded highly insulted.

"There he is now." Millie rose up to her knees on the vinyl booth and whipped her arms around as if she were on an aircraft carrier signaling in Tomcats. "Jamie!" she brayed. "Come on over and meet Kate's new fella!"

Jamie's face appeared in the kitchen's service window. Kate's head sank to the table with a thud.

When she gathered enough courage to look up, light-years later, Jamie was standing beside the table. There were no smashed chairs or thrown punches. There was only his face. It was as hard and still and pale as a marble statue. He kept his somber gaze glued to Millie, but Kate felt it blaze laserlike through her soul all the same. Immolation was no better than she deserved.

"Millie, let's not bother the customers," he said with no hint of emotion whatsoever as he hooked his hand under the older woman's arm.

Even Millie seemed cowed. "But Kate's not just another customer," she protested feebly.

"Yes, she is."

"Oh."

They left. Kate sat in miserable slump-shouldered silence.

Cotter coughed with delicacy. "Katrina, is there something you wish to tell me?"

She opened her mouth and shocked herself by saying, "I hate to be called Katrina."

"Then what do you prefer?"

Katy, she thought, but not from you. "Kate will do fine."

"Then, *Kate*, is there something you wish to tell me?" The worry lines on Cotter's forehead smoothed out. "Or was that woman simply a babbling drunk?"

He was giving her an out. Kate folded her hands on the table, knowing what he wanted to hear. But if she said it, what would that do to her integrity? She couldn't *deny* Jamie. That would be absolutely unconscionable.

"Jamie owns this place. He and I are—"

Cotter waved her off. "I believe I've already heard the gist of that part of it."

"I'm sorry."

He squeezed her hands between his. "No, I'm the one who's sorry. It seems I've moved too slow, Katri— Kate."

"I'm not—" She bit her lip. She wasn't . . . what? A loose woman, an easy bimbo? "I mean, I like slow." Or she used to. "Jamie and I aren't . . . attached, I guess you'd say." She gulped, trying to make herself swallow that one. "You're still . . ."

In the running, as far as Love Bytes goes.

Darn that Love Bytes. She'd been out of her gourd to start with it in the first place. And hugely stupid to have accepted another date with Cotter after . . . Jamie.

"I still have a chance with you?" Cotter prodded, although he didn't seem all that thrilled by the prospect.

He was merely circumspect about his feelings, Kate decided. Cotter was a gentleman, after all. Exactly the kind she'd thought she wanted. Why, then, was the desire to seek out Jamie so strong she could hardly keep her head from turning in his direction?

She couldn't, in fact. She slid out of the booth, mumbling, "Ladies' room," for Cotter's benefit. Which was where she ended up going. Every bar stool was filled and Manny was run off his feet. There was no sign of his boss.

The Ladies' was small, clean, tiled in salmon and teal. A faint scent of cigarette smoke hung in the air. Kate went to the sink and ran the water until it was icy cold. What she wanted to do was dunk her entire head under the faucet, but that reminded her of the time with Jamie at the pump. . . .

Everything reminded her of *some* time with Jamie.

She splashed her face, watching herself in the mirror. Her eyes were a huge, glazed, glistening green. She looked like a deer caught in the headlights, an instant *after* the impact.

She was dead in her tracks and it was all Love Bytes' fault.

The door opened. Kate hurriedly dried her hands with a sheet of brown paper from a push-button dispenser. A last glance in the mirror. "Finished in a mo—"

Jamie stood behind her.

"You had to rub my nose in it, didn't you?" His voice was harsh and raw.

He was no longer stone. Pain, jealousy and anger were etched on his features. Staring at him in the mirror, Kate understood how much she'd hurt him.

She gripped the edge of the sink, her breath coming in short, hard gasps. "I didn't want to come here." A weak excuse, and no real explanation.

"Yet you did."

"Cotter insisted."

"Well, then, that makes it all better."

"Jamie, please . . ." She turned, wavering on the heels of her sandals, intending to meet his eyes, but chickening out and staring instead at the intersecting yellow threads that ran through the gray plaid pattern of his shirt. Finally she whispered, "You didn't call."

She'd waited for three agonizing days.

His chest expanded and contracted like a bellows. "Neither did you."

"No," she admitted, shaking her head in misery. She hadn't been able to overcome her reserve to do so. *Girls do not call boys. Not nice girls.*

"I was waiting for you to decide what you want." His voice broke. "Maybe you have."

"No," she said again, pleading.

After a long moment of tense silence, Jamie shoved his hands into the pockets of linen trousers the color of lemon meringue, making a visible effort to relax. "So this Cotter's the big kahuna, huh?"

Kate's focus was finally jerked away from his wardrobe and up to his eyes. "What!"

"My main competition. Or am I so far out of the running it doesn't even matter?"

Competition. Was that what Love Bytes was? she wondered guiltily. No, it wasn't, not publicly, not as long as the subjects didn't *know* . . .

What exactly did Jamie know? Was his choice of phrase only coincidence?

Again.

Kate shook her head. No. She was imagining things.

He cleared his throat. "At least now I know what to say if I want to scare you off." His tone was softer, burred with regret.

She couldn't bear to have him believing she'd rejected his declaration of love out of hand. She stepped closer. "Jamie, you must know. What happened between us—it means a lot to me. More than I can put into words."

He stared. Clearly Kate was shaken. Her eyes were wide, vulnerable with her tentative offering. She would be devastated if he brushed her aside now, almost as devastated as he had been—still was—seeing her with the type of man Jamie knew he was not and never would be.

Was he crazy, or was there a still a chance, maybe a good chance, that he meant more to her than the Love Bytes rankings implied? He'd thought that their lovemaking would have proved that already, but stubborn Kate needed more convincing.

He touched a strand of her loose hair where it curled against her jaw. "I guess I shouldn't have moved so fast with you."

"No!" Her eyes flashed, then she caught herself. "What I mean is, no, I thought it was wonderful. But disturbing. You've become a...a fire in my blood." The confession was made with a whisper of dismay. And desire.

Male pride blossomed within him, but still he ached for just a little more. "You haven't mentioned love."

Gently she dropped her hands onto his chest. "I don't believe in love."

Cupping her jaw, lifting her face to his, he felt her quiver with emotion. "I've never met a woman who doesn't believe in love. How can you not?"

"I don't believe in the kind of love you're talking about," she whispered.

"And that is . . . ?"

She took a deep breath. "The easy-come, easy-go kind."

She might as well have stabbed him in the heart.

"I need more than infatuation, Jamie. I want a lifetime commitment."

Coming from any other woman, that would have been enough to make him run, fast, in the other direction, counting himself lucky to have escaped with his freedom intact. But with Kate, it was too late. She already had him—all of him—his heart, his soul, his bone and blood.

Knowing that at this point would definitely scare her off. So he kissed her instead, as sweetly as a schoolboy. "Don't go back to the professor."

"I can't be rude."

He started kissing her in earnest, knowing their physical attraction was one thing she couldn't deny.

"This is incredibly improper," she protested weakly.

She was wearing a crisp white cotton dress with little embroidered cutouts all around the scalloped neckline. He decided to kiss each tiny patch of skin they revealed. Half-moons, triangles, snippets and stars.

Kate was soon giggling, twisting and twitching under his lips, batting his hands away. He clasped her against him and kissed her soundly, his mouth quieting her until she was indolent and silky with bliss, murmuring deep in her throat, fingers gripping his shoulders.

Her lashes fluttered up when he released her. "Now you can go back to your date," he said, satisfied after one last nibble of her bottom lip. "But only if you promise not to let him touch you."

"Not after you," she pledged.

The door opened and two tipsy young women came into the bathroom. They laughed uproariously when they saw Jamie.

He escorted Kate out and sent her on her way. Her dress was wrinkled and her lips so lushly red it was obvious that she'd just been kissed. She didn't seem to realize it.

Jamie was betting that Cotter Coleman would.

PHASE TWO of Jamie's anti-Love Bytes campaign began the next day, when Gordon Hodge stopped in at Huckleberries to pick up his son. Suze's computer lesson had ten minutes to go, so Jamie offered Gordon a drink on the house while they waited for the kids to finish. He told Millie to take a hike. She bargained for a pack of cigarettes and slunk to a corner booth.

Roger and Rex were watching the Brewers beat the White Sox; they wouldn't have noticed an atomic blast. Whistler was busy in the kitchen, haranguing a supplier on the phone, and Carole, the only waitress on duty, was resting her feet and eating lunch leftovers.

Jamie was free to manipulate to his heart's content.

Gordon sat on a stool and asked for a light beer. No surprise there. After a minute of small talk, Jamie eased the conversation over to the end of summer school. Ergo, to Kate.

"That schoolteacher, Kate Mallory..." he said.

"She's supervising Gregory Gordon's science project. He's studying the effects of chlorophyll deprivation on the seedlings of various exotics."

"Fascinating." Jamie picked shriveled cherries and dried-up olives out of the fruit tray. "You two seemed kinda cozy during that field trip we all chaperoned."

"Kate's a fine woman."

"Yeah, and a fine figure of a woman, too."

Gordon's eyes seemed to swim behind the distortion of his thick lenses. He cleared his throat three times. "That's so."

"You date her?"

"I have. A couple of times."

"Hmm. Still seeing her?"

Gordon sipped his beer. "I'm not sure if she's all that interested. And I've been busy, myself," he hastened to add.

"I'm an inventor in my spare time. Got lots of projects going."

"Oh, really," Jamie said, nodding now and then as Gordon launched into a detailed description of the latest version of his battery-powered foot massagers. He was thinking of adding a hot oil dispenser and marketing them as Yuppie camping gear.

Subject #34GH's highest numbers had been in what Jamie had figured out was the Stability section of the Career category. He'd decided to attack strength, not weakness. The faster Gordon's numbers fell, the sooner his own would rise.

"If you don't mind my saying so, it sounds like you've got one job too many," he suggested once Gordon had wound down with a lament about not having enough time to devote to his other inventions. "Maybe you should give up one of them."

"I couldn't quit work on my foot massagers now, not when I'm so close to perfecting the prototype."

Jamie leaned both elbows on the bar. "So, bye-bye, Magnatech."

"Bye-bye, paycheck," Gordon countered. His forehead furrowed. "Fiscally that would be an unwise decision."

"Ahh." Jamie rubbed his chin. "How much you figure a patent's worth?"

"Depends on the device," Gordon said. "Say, a unique idea, something that catches on with the public..." He shrugged.

"Major moola?"

Gordon nodded eagerly. "You would not believe how much money Herbert Smeets made when he invented his Maximassagelator for back stress and lumbar rehabilitation."

"Well, hell, then, buddy, if I had your smarts, I'd be concentrating on those foot massagers. Think of the prestige of being known as the man with the million dollar patent. Kate would be awfully impressed." Jamie took a rag and started polishing the bar. "Yup, there's your ticket to the big time, Gordo. Not a piddly engineering job."

Gordon looked down at his beer through narrowed eyes. "You may be right."

Jamie tossed the rag into the sink and spread his hands, palms out. "Bartenders always are."

Downtown Belle Terre was all of three blocks long, a wide, sloping street canopied by tall elms. Monica was subtly working Kate toward the lavender awning of her favorite beauty salon. "You can't keep running around with your hair half red and half brown," she pointed out.

Kate stared in the window of the Bob's Baked Goods. The eclairs looked delicious. "I'm not sure that I want to have it colored again."

"Who said you have to?" Monica checked her wristwatch. "Andi can simply snip off the ends and—*voilà*, no more two-tone."

"But then I'd be a redhead."

Monica rolled her eyes. "Imagine that!"

Kate could, for the first time in a decade. That was the problem. "I don't have an appointment. All the stylists are probably busy."

"Trust me, they'll take you." Monica had made sure of that when she'd set it up.

"I do think Jamie actually prefers red hair . . ."

"Then that decides it." The door chimes tinkled as Monica pushed Kate inside the salon, waving to Andi, a stylist whose own tri-tone—magenta, black and blue—punk style did not inspire Kate's confidence. Andi whipped out a plastic cape and plopped Kate into the shampoo chair before she could protest.

A few minutes later, she was staring at her wet head in the mirror while Andi circled her, bracelets jingling and scissors snipping. Kate shut her eyes and prayed.

Monica lounged in the neighboring chair, indulging herself in a manicure. "A bit shorter, Andi," she directed. Kate winced as a hank of damp hair fell into her lap. "Don't worry, Kate, you'll be gorgeous."

"Gorgeous," agreed Andi.

"Jamie will go wild when he sees you," Monica promised.

"Wild," said Andi, with another *snip-snip-snip*.

"He's already wild enough," muttered Kate.

Monica selected Persimmon Pearlescence for her nails. "I wish Ed would catch some of that. Instead it's only my kids who drive me wild and a lot of good that does my libido."

"No good," Andi clucked.

Kate caught Monica's eye in the mirror. "Your daughter is friendly with Jamie's, isn't she?"

"Sure. Kirsten and Suzannah have been buddies since kindergarten."

"What do you think of her?"

"Basically, she's a good kid."

"Basically," murmured Andi.

"But?" Kate persisted.

Monica sighed. "What do you want me to say? Does this have something to do with Love By—"

Kate spun her chair around and quieted Monica with a meaningful glare. "Whoopsie," Andi scolded, yanking the scissors away as a tuft of red-tinged hair fell to the floor.

"Shorter," she and Monica said in unison. "Jinx!" They laughed girlishly.

"Please don't mention you-know-what," said Kate.

Monica narrowed her eyes. "You're downgrading Jamie simply because his daughter is free-spirited," she accused. "Your stodgy parents may have raised you to be a timid little mouse, but that's no reason for you to let their prejudices influence Jamie's score."

"But Parenting Potential is an important category in—". Kate darted a glance at Andi "—you-know-what," she finished lamely. "Suzannah isn't just spirited. She's undisciplined. That's Jamie's fault."

"Then I'm a bad mother, too."

"I didn't say that."

"No? T.J. smashed up the family car the first week he had his learner's permit. Kirsten flunked your natural science class and by the smell in her room I suspect she's experimenting with cigarettes. Violet's still well-behaved, but then she's only eight. Give the kid a few years and we'll see."

Earnestly, Kate leaned toward Monica, having completely forgotten about her ongoing haircut. "But T.J. took a part-time job to pay for the repairs, and Kirsten is an honors student in English. You're a great mother, Monica. Anyone who knows you would say so."

Monica let that sink into Kate's brain before she spoke again. "You're absolutely correct. Making snap judgements just doesn't work, does it? A person's got to look at the big picture, and even then keep in mind that it's still not three-dimensional."

After a long moment of inner struggle, Kate nodded. "Touché."

"Touché," chimed Andi as she whipped off the plastic cape.

Kate gaped at the reflection of her shorn, bedraggled head.

Monica and Andi turned from the mirror as one. "Blow dryer," they announced together.

"Jinx," said Kate.

8

KATE STAYED TO HERSELF for a couple of days, trying to get used to her new redheaded reflection in the mirror. When that didn't work so well—probably because she spent more time avoiding the mirror than studying it—she decided to face the music at Huckleberries. Since she had a date with Jamie anyway, she put in an appearance near closing time on Sunday afternoon, once she was sure the lunch crowd had cleared out.

Reminding herself that being a redhead carried with it certain entitlements, such as having the boldness to be the center of attention, she swallowed hard, stuck her chin in the air and banged through the bar's swinging doors pretending to be everything that she was not. Or *thought* she wasn't. On that question, she was no longer sure.

Since the bar was nearly empty, the reaction to the new Kate wasn't all that it could have been, and Kate, surprised, admitted to herself that she was actually disappointed.

She halted in the middle of the floor. Roger and Rex didn't glance away from the baseball game. The only other customers, Millie and Cecil, were huddled in a booth, talking and holding hands. Millie smiled and Cecil doffed his beret distractedly before returning to their cozy confab.

Wilting, Kate went over to the bar and dropped onto her usual stool. She certainly *felt* different, inside and out, so why wasn't anyone noticing? What a letdown.

Then Jamie came whistling from the kitchen.

He stopped dead, his lips pursed on a silenced note. His dark red brows arched. "*Kate?*"

Now that was more like it. Kate hugged herself and said, with a jaunty shake of her head so her hair swung attractively. "It's me."

He approached with caution. "It *is* you."

She brushed the ends of the short, angled cut, aware of the soft red glow of color reflected in the mirror behind the bar. "It's only a haircut," she said, even though they both knew it was much more than that.

"Yeah, sure. That's what Delilah said to Samson."

Suddenly Kate felt bashful again. Employing the personality of a redhead was going to take some getting used to. "Do you like it?" she whispered.

Jamie came closer and put both of his hands to her head. He stroked her hair, threading his fingers through it, brushing it off her forehead, rubbing a strand beneath his thumb like a connoisseur. "I think it's . . . you. Gorgeously."

"I'm still not sure about that."

He smiled. "You will be."

"What does that mean—"

Millie chose that moment to interrupt. She slapped her hands on the bar and blared, "Hidey-hidey-ho, Carrot-top!"

Kate winced. "Afternoon, Millie." Her gaze slid back to Jamie. He seemed sort of dazed by her transformation, but his smile was pure bliss. Nice. Having such an effect on men was one part of being a redhead that she might really take to.

Particularly if the man was Jamie.

Millie plopped onto a stool. "Well, redheads, congratulations are in order. I'm getting hitched!"

Kate responded without actually looking away from Jamie. "That's great, Millie. Best wishes."

"Yup, never thought I'd find a man who I'd wanna stay married to, but after fifty-two years, Cecil finally showed up."

Jamie blinked. "Fifty-eight years."

"Picky, picky," Millie sniped. She shot Jamie a sly look. "Say, Huck, doesn't my big announcement rate a round on the house?"

"Congratulations, congratulations," Roger and Rex instantly chimed, holding out their mugs. Jamie woke up enough to fill them from the tap. He asked Kate if she wanted an espresso—or something.

That something was a strawberry margarita, she was certain, and decided on the espresso. For the moment.

Jamie was still smiling, his attention returning again and again to Kate's red hair as he prepared their drinks. "Millie, as a first-time bride, I'm sure you'll want to stick to something nontoxic." Smug, he set a tomato-colored drink garnished with a celery stalk and a paper parasol before the older woman.

She crinkled her nose. "A Virgin Mary? I don't think so!"

Roger and Rex thought that was hilarious.

"Millie, love, get back over here. We haven't discussed flowers," called Cecil from the booth where he was scribbling in a tiny notebook, a beret tilted rakishly across his thinning silver hair. "And what sort of music shall we have at the reception?"

Millie took the Virgin Mary with her. "I vote for Venus flytraps and honky-tonk," she hollered. "Haw! Haw! Haw!"

Kate rested both elbows on the brass handrail and put her chin on her folded hands to watch Jamie move back and forth between the espresso machine, the beer cooler and the lined-up bottles in the speed rack. Technically, she should be taking mental notes for Love Bytes on how smoothly he ran the bar, how he handled difficult customers with tact and appeared to easily shoulder the responsibility of owning his own business. But why not just enjoy herself?

"So Millie is fifty-eight," she commented when Jamie paused to total the Sunday receipts and count the cash drawer. "I guess I thought she was older."

"She's led a hard life."

"It's nice of you to watch out for her." That would earn him a few Human Kindness points, if she had such a category.

Jamie wrapped a roll of quarters. "Someone's got to."

"Kitchen's closing," Whistler yelled out the pass-through. "Anyone want the last of the bean soup?"

"Please, Grandpa, no more dishes!" wailed Suzannah, out of sight, splashing in the sink.

"I'll give it to Cecil and Millie. Maybe some hot food in their stomachs will keep 'em sober enough so they won't go overboard celebrating their engagement." Jamie took the bowls of soup, and as he passed Kate he told her, "Suze is putting in a few free hours of kitchen work as punishment for computer hacking."

Hacking? wondered Kate. While many of her students were amazingly adept with computers, she hadn't pegged Suzannah as the type. She was adding another black mark to the girl's record when she remembered how Monica had lectured her at the salon about leaping to conclusions. Kate decided to wait until she knew the whole story. It could have been a harmless prank.

Love Bytes was turning into a real education. Analyzing what personality traits and values were most important had made her aware of certain qualities in herself, as well as others. For one, she wasn't always as objective as she'd prided herself on being. And she'd also discovered her

stubborn streak; she refused to trash all her work on Love
Bytes simply because of a bad—okay, raging—case of infatuation.

A case from which she wished she'd never be cured.

Huckleberries cleared out. Kate went to help Suzannah
put the chairs up on the tables for sweeping. Jamie and
Whistler were clanking on something in the kitchen when
Suzannah glanced sidelong past the broom handle and said,
"Nice hair."

For an instant, Kate thought the girl was being sarcastic.
Then she decided that her reaction was just a defensive
posture left over from her childhood. "Thanks. Would you
believe it's my real color?"

Suzannah tilted her head, her tongue making a bump in
her cheek. "Red hair rules."

"Yeah." Kate touched the soft feathery wisps that framed
her face. "But I used to hate it."

"So'd I. Then I saw a picture of—" Suzannah tossed her
hair like a girl in a shampoo ad "—Rachel Hunter, the su-
permodel. Before Rod Stewart made her go blond. The
jerk!"

They commiserated over poor Anne of Green Gables
with her red braids and freckles. Suzannah recalled that
Pippi Longstocking was similarly tressed and that she'd had
loads of fun. Kate didn't know Pippi, but she listed Kath-
arine Hepburn as a famous redhead. Suzannah was adding
The Little Mermaid to the roster when Whistler came out
to hurry them along. Suzannah was sleeping at her grand-
parent's house that night.

Kate and Jamie locked up Huckleberries, went to the
video store and had a friendly argument over what to rent,
stopped to pick up a few groceries and finally arrived at
Kate's house. Boris chased them down the sidewalk, then
patrolled the fence for fifteen minutes after they'd closed the

All Shook Up

gate, nipping and yapping at the overhanging branches of the apple tree.

Feeling shy about sharing the kitchen—the scene of the crime, so to speak—Kate asked Jamie to set the patio table and pour the wine while she hurried through dinner preparations. Knowing exactly what she was avoiding, he grinned wickedly but acquiesced without a word of protest.

It was a beautiful summer evening. The long, low rays of the setting sun slanted across the garden to reach Kate's round bistro table, glancing off the silver and pooling on the plain white china. The wine glittered with tiny golden bubbles.

She placed two shallow bowls of cold pale green cantaloupe soup on the table. "So white wine is acceptable on occasion?"

"It has qualities I've come to appreciate," Jamie admitted.

He started talking about Whistler's homemade wine, his voice a low murmur that prickled right up Kate's spine and did strange things to her tongue. Hmm, yes, there was something wrong with her tongue. It was warm and heavy and too big for her mouth. Maybe not for Jamie's, she thought with an inner giggle, and curled it around a spoonful of soup.

They had thin slices of chicken breast and prosciutto with melon and crispy rounds of Italian bread. A tangy deli salad. More wine. Decadently rich Black Forest cake for dessert, mined with dark sweet cherries. Their conversation was lazy and quiet, interspersed with long silences.

The warm summer twilight arrived. The sky had deepened from a faded blue tinged with pink to mauve to starsprinkled purple. Jamie's left hand rested on the tabletop, his forefinger idly stroking the stem of one of the goblets.

Kate was tingling with a corresponding sensation, the thrill ebbing and flowing with each small flick of his fingertip. She tilted her head far back and let her mind go free until it was swirling with stars and summer and the sweet memory of Jamie's kiss.

His lips touched the white arch of her throat. "My beautiful redhead," he whispered.

She preened under his soft caress and said "Yes . . ." without thinking.

His hands skimmed her body as lightly as the breeze. "My love."

A soft sigh escaped her lips as she turned in her slatted chair, reaching for him. The light from the carriage lamp near the door bathed her face when she lifted it, her eyes searching his as she tried to find the proper words to tell him how she felt.

"Shh." Jamie touched his fingers to her lips. "You don't have to speak." His mouth joined his fingers, and he kissed her with loving reassurance, his lips stroking like silken feathers on hers, his fingers trembling as if touching her were touching a miracle. Kate tasted the hot sting of tears at the back of her throat. Jamie had courage, and faith in their future; she had only worries and doubts and dreams. Yet she wanted him, even more than she wanted to weep.

"We should go inside," he murmured.

She gulped air and tears. "Yes . . ."

Jamie drew away and picked up several dishes. "We did rent that movie."

She'd forgotten. They'd settled on *Sabrina*, the remake with Harrison Ford. Kate stared at the table, her pulse flickering like the flame in the hurricane lamp she'd lit at the fall of dusk. Lifting the glass chimney, she extinguished the wick.

"Yes, the movie," she said. "I missed it when it was in theaters last winter." She'd missed out on a lot of things because of her narrow focus.

Kate insisted they leave the dishes for tomorrow. She asked Jamie if he wanted popcorn. He said he couldn't eat another bite, so they went into the living room, where the television and VCR were tucked into a low walnut credenza with heavy carved doors and hammered brass fixtures. Jamie teased her about the meager size of her TV screen and Kate confessed that she hadn't bought a VCR until Monica had convinced her that she was the last person in all of Western civilization without one. Although she wasn't yet caught up on all of Hollywood, she had discovered Harrison Ford.

Jamie couldn't concentrate on *Sabrina*, not with Kate beside him on the settee, her wispy skirt smoothed across her curled legs and her emerald eyes glowing in the light of the television screen. He watched her thick lashes sweep down to kiss her cheeks when she blinked, and smiled as she kept unconsciously putting her hand to the nape of her neck, touching the newly revealed skin, her fingers brushing across the blunt ends of her angled haircut. A silky wave of it fell across her left eye and she blew it back with an impatient puff of air out of the side of her mouth.

He ached to kiss that mouth. Yearned to stroke that hair, caress that nape.

Kate turned to him as if his thoughts had been audible. She smiled curiously, her eyebrows going up. "The movie's over."

"Oh, yeah." Jamie swallowed. Remembering that he had the remote control, he clicked the TV off. The room was heavy with silence, broken only by the whir of the rewinding cassette.

Boris barked outside and Kate turned her face away again. "That horrible dog," she said, getting up to part the moss green velvet drapes and peer out at the dark shrubbery shivering in the wind. Moonlight silvered the lace undercurtains, tracing an intricate pattern across her face.

"I'm wondering if you're going to invite me upstairs," Jamie said suddenly, unwilling to wait for her to make the overture. The velvet drape slipped from her fingers. "Or do you prefer to make love down here?"

Keeping me unofficial, he added in his mind. *Keeping me out of your private places, and out of your stubborn heart.*

The question was a test of sorts. Was he a dalliance, or was he more . . . ?

Kate had drawn a deep breath and squared her shoulders. She walked straight out of the room. Jamie followed her to the hallway, where the narrow dark wood staircase curved in on itself on the way to the second floor. She glanced at the door—his hopes plummeted like a roller coaster—then up the stairs, a look of resolve on her lovely face.

"Upstairs," she said. Firmly.

The roller coaster soared. "To the bedroom?"

"Yes." Her glance was shy. "Or did you have something more exotic in mind?"

He encircled her with his arms and dropped kisses over her hair. "Conventional can be nice, too." Was he crazy or did her shampoo smell like strawberries? "I like your hair, Katy," he whispered into her ear, licking the back of it with the tip of his tongue.

She shivered. "You already told me." Her hand went to her nape again, a reflex.

"A big change for you, hmm?"

"I'm still not sure about the color. Is it garish?"

He was hugging her tight. "I wish you knew how beautiful you are."

Kate turned in his arms and kissed him. "When I'm with you, I feel beautiful. Isn't that good enough?"

No, he thought, but offered her a quirky grin. "Then let's go upstairs and I'll make you feel absolutely gorgeous."

"SO THIS IS YOUR COMPUTER," he said, eyeing the unassuming machine placed on a Queen Anne writing desk in her small upstairs office.

Kate laughed. "You say that as if it's momentous."

"Do you, uh, hook up with the school computers?" he asked, uncertain of the correct terminology. He knew for a fact that Kate did. When confronted, Suze had confessed how she'd persuaded Gregory Gordon to sneak into the school computer records so she could check her summer school grade. She'd made loud noises about how unfair it was to be punished for a scheme that hadn't even worked.

It had worked out beautifully for Jamie; it had given him Love Bytes. Probably a pious role model of a father wouldn't have taken advantage of that fact, but, hey, he'd never claimed to be one. He had, however, kept his own breach of conduct to himself, and gone easier on Suze than he might have, otherwise.

"Yes," Kate said, tapping the modem. "I work both at home and at the school, so it's convenient to telecommunicate between the two."

"Using passwords?"

"Right. The school's computer system has one, and I have a personal password for my own files. It's very secure."

Not from a techno-nerd under the influence of his first teenage crush, Jamie thought. He wondered how Kate would react if she knew he'd seen a printout of her Love Bytes project. At first, he'd thought it was a very elaborate version of the one-to-ten ratings system, but after reading through it several times and decoding most of the notations, he'd come to believe that Love Bytes was a husband-hunting tool. Kate had practically admitted as much when she'd said she intended to marry...soon.

Soon. Jamie was a little worried about that. What if he had only a matter of days to ensure that his rank rose to number one?

And what would happen if he was successful? Should he confess that he'd known all along? Or keep quiet, even though he already felt guilty enough about invading her privacy?

Maybe he should slap a ring on her finger and marry her quickly, before she realized just how ridiculous choosing a husband by computer actually was.

Oh, Katy, he thought. *For a brainy schoolteacher, you're really kind of dense.*

"And what are these?" he said, pointing at random to a row of empty glass jars on a shelf. The office had a steeply slanting ceiling punched with a tiny curved eyebrow window, another small paned window on the end wall, full bookshelves without an inch of space to spare, a rocking chair and a big round rag rug on the plank floor.

"In the spring, those bottles held my imagoes and chrysalides. My students and I breed butterflies and various insects so they can experience the miracle of metamorphosis..." Kate's voice trailed off. She wasn't in the mood for a lecture about hatching cocoons.

She didn't understand why Jamie had detoured into her office on the way to the bedroom, or why he was so interested in her computer. Thank heaven her hard copy of Love Bytes was neatly stashed away in the desk drawer—including the latest printout in which Jamie had risen all the way up to the seventh position. Seventh with a bullet.

"Excuse me," Kate blurted, and ran to the bathroom. She locked herself in, suddenly stricken with panic. What was she doing? If this was all just research for Love Bytes, making love to Jamie a second time made no sense at all. She already had plenty of data on that facet of their relationship—plenty!

She leaned back against the door. No, what was happening between them could no longer be called research. It was . . . *Love*, a voice inside her heart whispered. Or simply infatuation masquerading as love, her logical brain replied.

That was the scientific explanation. But her heart hung on to the other. For once in her life Kate wanted to give in to emotion and impulse.

She opened the door to her bedroom. Jamie had lit several candles. The flames cast a flickering light over the periwinkle-blue slanted ceilings and threw deep shadows into the peaked dormer nook that held her pine four-poster bed. They backlit Jamie's head with a fiery halo, tipped his auburn hair with threads of gold.

Nervously Kate fumbled with the folds of her long skirt as she kicked off her espadrilles. When Jamie's shoes instantly joined hers on the carpet, she laughed a little and lifted her hands, letting her fingers toy with the top button of her black silk blouse.

He followed suit, popping the first few buttons of his shirt until she could see a tantalizing slash of golden brown skin. It reminded her of the way he'd once stripped for her at Huckleberries.

"May I do that for you?" she asked, her eyes large and her voice small.

He spread his hands. "Be my guest."

Kate came forward and slid the side of her hand down the buttoned seam, revealing more of his chest, the flat bands of hard muscles, the V of paprika-colored fuzz between them, the sculpted span of his shoulders. The warm scent of his skin filled her nostrils as she dropped his shirt to the carpet. With a sigh hovering on her lips, she kissed the lovely shadowed hollow between his shoulder and chest. He tasted faintly of spicy soap or aftershave.

His hands were gathering up the tiny pleats of her skirt, reaching past the wadded gauzy fabric to cup the curves of her derriere. "Wait," Kate scolded. She saw his eyes flash when he goosed her, then dance at her openmouthed flinch. Playfully she slapped his chest. "I said wait!"

She didn't make him wait long. Her hands dropped to his belt and more or less ripped it open, then yanked down his zipper with an audible *ziiip* of haste. The loose trousers slid down his sturdy legs with a soft whoosh; a pair of black silk boxers patterned with tiny red hearts pierced by metallic gold arrows soon followed.

"At least these shorts don't say 'Home of the Whopper'," she commented, pretending a sigh that turned to a deep-throated purr when she looked down and realized that no such label was required.

"I do have a pair of those," he murmured, reaching out to caress her wavy cap of golden red hair.

"You would."

"They also glow in the dark. I'll wear them for you next time."

Kate lunged for him, laughing, and kissed him hard, her mouth open and her tongue thrusting. He kissed her back just as fiercely, and the intensity of the moment built until it was almost blinding. The blurry candle flames danced, magnifying larger and larger until the room seemed to be on fire. Even when her eyes closed Kate could see the flames flickering on her inner lids as if she was burning up from the inside out.

"Now is it my turn to undress you?" Jamie was already running his palms down her body, snagging the hem of her paper-thin, copper-colored skirt, lifting it to bare her legs.

She nodded, keeping her eyes closed.

Nuzzling her neck, Jamie slipped around behind her. His arms were looped at her waist, his hips and thighs molded against hers, swaying, making her sway, too, until they'd rocked back and forth in a swoony half circle to face the cheval glass in the corner of the bedroom.

"Open your eyes, Katy," he whispered into her ear.

She opened them a slit, saw the full-length mirror and closed them tight again, shaking her head. "Don't make me. I can't look, I'm too shy."

"You're beautiful. Open your eyes and see," he coaxed. "See how beautiful you are."

He'd unbuttoned the waistband of her skirt as he spoke and now pushed it past her hips so it pooled on the floor in a spiraled pattern of narrow broomstick pleats. Kate's eyelids flashed open in breath-held surprise when he slowly slipped her frilled black satin tap pants down her thighs and left them curled at her ankles.

She tilted her head back against his shoulder and stared through her lashes at the shadowy image of herself, clad only in a blouse. "Is it me?" she asked, abashed and aroused.

"Oh, yes, it's you, Katy," Jamie said. "The woman I love."

Overwhelmed, she tried to turn away, but Jamie held her tight. "Look, look," he breathed. "Look how beautiful."

Erotic, she thought, watching in the mirror as he unbuttoned the black blouse, his hands stunningly masculine, but also gentle as they stripped her, easing the blouse down her arms. The whisper of silk was enticing in the silent room.

"Ohhh," she moaned when his hands came up again from behind to cradle her aching breasts, his thumbs rubbing at her stiff nipples through the black satin bra. She was all liquid and warm inside, all acute sensation out.

"Beautiful," he said again as he flicked the snaps of the bra and peeled the cups back, letting her breasts swing free like exotic ripe fruit. He put his hands around her waist and simply held her again, both of them swaying with pleasure, swimming with desire. "Look."

Kate truly looked at herself at last. The sheen of candlelight glowed on her skin, turning it peachy gold and smooth as a baby's. Her legs were long, her thighs shapely, the red furred triangle between them shockingly licentious as Jamie framed it with his splayed fingers. His hands rose to her breasts, lifting them, squeezing and fondling as he kissed her stylish short red hair and teased his tongue across the slope of her shoulder and then Kate couldn't look anymore. She *was* ablaze, every scorched nerve ending so excruciatingly sensitized her body screamed where Jamie touched it and screamed even louder where he didn't.

He brought her to the bed and laid her down upon it. Wild-eyed and eager, she parted her thighs even before he knelt between them, distended and enormous, filling her with his gliding thrust . . . filling her with rapture.

And the words she said to him, when his mouth was hot and wet on hers and their rhythm had peaked and the torrents of pleasure crashed through her, the words she said out of pure instinct were, "I love you."

"I'VE THOUGHT OF A JOKE."

Jamie lifted the blue-gold and rose patchwork quilt to find Kate's face, flushed and mischievous. "Let's hear it," he said, cozily snuggling her to his side.

She giggled to herself. "Okay. Here it is. What do Kate Mallory and the Huckleberries' cash register have in common?"

"Ahhh . . ." he said, thinking. "I give up."

"So soon?"

"Tell me," he said, sternly commanding.

"All right. The answer is—" She was quivering with barely withheld self-congratulations for her humor. "They both go *ka-ching* when Jamie presses the right button!" She burst into giddy laughter, flopping around on the bed like a landed fish.

"Katrina Mallory!" Jamie said with a gleeful shout. He pulled her over on top of him. "I'm appalled."

She chortled something unintelligible against his chest.

"You're so naughty," he reproached.

She lifted her head, shaking her hair out of her eyes. "Oh, you're way worse, Mr. Flying Pigs Boxer Shorts, Mr. Ice Cube Down My Panties."

He slapped her naked bottom. "Didn't cool you off any, did it?"

She stuck out her tongue.

Jamie's upper lip curled as he slipped the flat of his hand between her thighs. "Wanna play Button, Button?" he asked, and watched her eyes go round with surprise. Seconds later, surprise turned to delight.

TWENTY MINUTES LATER Kate's head again emerged from under the patchwork quilt. She did an earthworm wiggle up to the pillows, where she collapsed, prone, spread-eagle and still breathing hard. "Very nice," she said to Jamie's feet.

He shifted them off the pillow, hunching on all fours under the quilt as he changed position and plopped down beside Kate. "My feet or my—"

"Good heavens, you're irrepressible." She sighed with total satiety. "And I'm extremely grateful."

"Also extremely welcome." Jamie kissed her, got out of bed, blew out the candle stubs and went into the bathroom. When he came back a few minutes later, Kate was propped up on the pillows, the sheet and quilt neatly folded under her armpits, her tousled hair finger-combed back to respectability. A ginger jar lamp cast a circle of light on the pine nightstand.

Her lashes were lowered modestly as he slid back into bed. "Don't poop out on me now," he said.

Her lips twitched. "Poop?"

"You know what I mean." With his arms around her, he nuzzled her neck. "I'm going to stay in love with you, even afterward, so don't you dare poop out on me." He paused significantly, waiting for her to respond in kind.

She hesitated. "Okay, answer me this. You love me when I'm Katy, but what about when I'm 'teach'? Or just plain Kate? Because I am, you know, most of the time. This—" she gestured at the bed "—this is the out of the ordinary me."

At least she'd admitted that it was a *part* of her. "Not out of the ordinary, Kate. Just private." Jamie smiled. "Strictly private, between you and me."

Then he remembered her rate-a-date project and the smile faded. He was definitely going to have to do something about Love Bytes. Finish it off once and for all.

"I love every part of you, Katrina Mallory," he vowed. "Every inch, every nickname, every last red hair on your head. How's that for an answer? Good enough?"

"Plenty good." She kissed his cheek, but that was all. No 'I love you, too.'

He frowned. Saying something in the heat of the moment didn't count, not permanently.

"Do you want another child?" Kate asked suddenly.

He was jolted. "Are you trying to tell me something?"

"No! I mean, we did use protection and it's only been a week or so, since . . . so no, of course I'm not preg—I was only asking, that's all."

"Why?"

"Curiosity? There's a lot I don't know about you, and I . . ."

Want to complete the dossier on #35JF, he silently supplied. "The truth is, I haven't thought about it. Suze is a handful on her own, and exactly where is this new baby supposed to come from anyhow?" His tone was the teensiest bit nasty. Thinking about Kate judging, labeling and grading him was about as much fun as chewing glass.

"Some anonymous woman?" he said. "Or a wife—otherwise known as the old ball and chain." He started to laugh at his lame joke, but stopped when he saw Kate's face.

She put her head in her hands. "Sorry I brought the subject up."

Jamie wanted to put his own head on the chopping block. Oh, he was really Mr. Smooth, wasn't he? Even though he knew that fantastic sex—even mediocre sex—tended to put women into a snuggly, domestic, heart-to-heart kind of mood, he just couldn't be bothered to keep his wiseass remarks to himself.

"Listen, Kate," he said. "You're the first woman I've loved since Sunny, and I'm feeling kind of—" He bit off the word *uncertain*. Did he say what he thought she wanted to hear, in order to earn a high Love Bytes score, or did he tell the strict truth? And was it possible that the two choices were one and the same . . . ? *What a concept.*

Softly Kate cleared her throat. "I guess your wife was so perfect she ruined you for other women."

Jamie dropped back against the pillows, his mind racing. "Actually, no." He might have used that as an excuse with other women, but not with Kate.

"Don't get me wrong. Of course I loved Sunny, but it's been ten years since her death and, to be frank, I've come to realize that Whistler and Charity were a big part of why our marriage worked. They seemed to know how to keep Sunny grounded without clipping her wings. And they welcomed me into the family with open arms, even though they were disappointed about us marrying so young. When Suze came along, I figured our family was complete. We were safe and solid."

He was silent for a long while, then added, "And that was what I needed, maybe even more than I wanted to marry Sunny just for herself. If you can separate the two, which you probably can't."

"I think I understand," Kate said quietly.

"I'd never had any permanence in my life up to then," he explained. "My mother's an alcoholic. We moved from town to town, from bar to bar, from temporary job to unemployment to welfare. I didn't know my father. Not even his name."

Kate took his fisted hand and peppered kisses across the knuckles until they unclenched. "We have more in common than I first thought."

"Is that so? I thought you grew up with all the advantages."

"Of the material and intellectual sort, yes." She kissed his palm more slowly and pressed it to her cheek as she tilted her head to look at him, her lips soft, pink, alluring. "But I always wanted to be a part of a normal, loving, responsive family. Being how I am, I'd planned to use my brain power to create my own."

Starting with a husband of the first rank, Jamie thought. He knew she was talking about Love Bytes.

Kate continued. "For the longest time I thought this potential family had to be the All-American ideal. I didn't intend to settle for anything less than perfection." She moved her cheek against his palm. "But not anymore."

"Oh," Jamie said, wanting to take her in his arms. The problem was that he'd hate to be what she "settled" for.

Kate came into his arms on her own. "And I do love you, Jamie," she confessed in a low whisper. He brushed his lips along the crown of her hair, the scent of strawberries hovering in the air. "I just need some time to figure out what that means to me. Is that okay with you?"

What could he say but yes?

9

IN THE MORNING, Jamie was gone.

Awakening to find herself naked and alone in the bed, Kate couldn't believe it at first. She couldn't believe that he'd walk out on her without a word. Not after last night. She leapt up and dashed around the bedroom, looking for a note, a sign, *something*.

Nothing.

That was what came from telling a man you loved him.

Slipping into a robe on the fly, she ran downstairs, but again there was nothing. Only *Sabrina*, rewound in the VCR, and three-quarters of a Black Forest triple-decker cake in the kitchen. With a cry of "Just desserts!" Kate picked it up and threw it in the trash can, cake plate and all. It was the rash act of an impulsive, hotheaded woman and it gave her only a fleeting sense of satisfaction.

"Calm down, Kate," she muttered, stomping back up the stairs. "Stay rational. Use your common sense." It was her parents' mantra.

But even logically thinking through Jamie's disappearance didn't help. It wasn't as if he had to get to work early. His late hours at Huckleberries were one of the factors that had kept his Career score low. Cotter's schedule, for instance, matched so advantageously with her own. Family togetherness would be no problem with #27CC and their mutual long summer vacations.

And Jamie had conveniently stashed Suzannah with her grandparents, so going home to his daughter was no excuse, either. It could be that he'd often used Charity as a baby-sitter in order to have privacy with his various floozies—something Kate couldn't bear thinking about if she hadn't been forced to for the sake of Love Bytes. By contrast, #15OP, the electrician with four kids, had said he'd sacrifice anything for his brood—even his time with Kate.

Maybe Otto Plimpton wasn't such a good example, Kate admitted as she stripped the sheets off the bed, balled them up and tossed them toward the door. She'd decided that Otto was looking for a mother for his children, not a wife.

Okay, then, look at #34GH. Gordon Hodge was thoroughly reliable, steady and solid as they came. If she'd invited Gordon into her bed last night, she could've good and well counted on him still being there in the morning. But not Jamie, oh, no, not Jamie. He wasn't one to be linked to a ball and chain!

Kate threw the pillows across the room in frustration. She wasn't used to feeling like this. So edgy and wired and . . . well, needy. It wasn't like her.

But it was like Katy, she thought, catching a glimpse of herself in the cheval mirror. She looked away from the obvious nudity under her loosened robe. Then she looked back again, relentlessly drawn by her lascivious reflection. Her cheeks were pink, her lips bee-stung. When the lapels of the robe widened another inch she couldn't help but notice that her breasts bore love bites of their own.

"I am Katy," she whispered to her mirror image. "And I am in love with a man who doesn't even have the courtesy to stay the night."

"Damn you, Jamie!" she railed, turning away from the blasted mirror. For the first time in her life she'd wakened in the mood for morning-after loving and cuddling and sweet talking. And had received a big zero in response. According to hipper women than she, modern men did have a tendency to cut and run before dawn arrived. Jamie might have regretted what he'd told her in the dark of night. Maybe he had decided to get while the getting was good.

"The jerk," she said.

No, not a jerk. Just a guy. Just another guy, date number one thousand, one hundred and sixty-five, give or take. Or #35JF, to be precise.

Somewhere in her heart Kate knew it was unfair to do so when she was in such a mood, but she went into her office, fired up the computer and began converting her latest impressions into hard data for Jamie's Love Bytes file.

With a gesture of impatience, she wrapped the robe over her pinkened, sensitive breasts. Love bites, indeed!

PROFESSOR COTTER COLEMAN was sitting at the bar when Jamie walked into Huckleberries early that afternoon. Jamie had called Kate once before he'd snatched a quick nap on his couch, then twice after waking and shaving. Reaching the answering machine all three times, he'd hung up without leaving a message. He wasn't going to explain to a machine why he'd left her house—and bed—in the middle of the night.

He shrugged and took a tumbler from the overhead rack and poured a drink from the jug of orange juice they kept on hand for mixed drinks. Since he hadn't reached Kate on the phone, he had more time to find the words to explain his current family situation. He'd tell her the next time he saw her, which he figured would be soon enough, anyway. There would be no more waiting around while she waffled over the Love Bytes rankings.

Love Bytes. Jamie looked at Cotter over the lip of his glass as he drained the orange juice. Time to wrap things up there, even if Kate had seemed mostly convinced of their suitability last night.

Just a little insurance, he decided, approaching the good professor. "Can I warm that up for you?" he asked.

Cotter nudged his latte across the bar. "You may."

Jamie wondered why Cotter was sitting in Huckleberries at 1:15 in the afternoon. "You're Cotter Coleman," he said, returning the coffee cup.

Cotter took a hot gulp of the latte. "And you're the bartender. Is it . . . James?"

"Jamie Flynn. I own the place."

"Ah, yes." Cotter's chiseled lips pursed. "I believe you're also the man who's been making time with my Katrina on the sly."

"Not on the sly," Jamie said flatly. *And not your Katrina.*

"I thought she was a woman of virtue. A woman of value—"

"What makes you say she isn't?" Jamie snapped.

Cotter ignored the question. "Here I was behaving as such a gentleman, treating Katrina with kid gloves, and along comes a rogue—" he swept Jamie from head to toe with his haughty gaze "—such as yourself and—and—*punches her doughnut!*"

Jamie blinked, startled, until he recognized Millie's phrase. "You've got to strike while the iron's hot, man," he said, wondering where the professor was going with this. Was he spoiling for a fight? If so, it wouldn't be the first bar fight Jamie had won, but allowing it to happen would set a bad precedent for his rowdier clientele.

Fortunately Cotter backed off. "My own fault," he mumbled into his drink. He looked up, evaluating Jamie through narrowed eyes. "Have you ever heard of the good girl, bad girl complex?"

"I guess." Jamie was still wary.

"I confess I am a sufferer," Cotter said. "The simple truth is that I'm not drawn, physically, you understand, to a gentlewoman like Kate."

Jamie nodded, thinking that the good professor had rocks for brains, but, hey, that was Cotter's loss. And Jamie's gain.

Cotter's eyes shifted. "I am attracted to another type of woman altogether."

Jamie followed the direction of Cotter's gaze. Yvette, the blowsy blond softball groupie, was eating lunch at one of the tables. Cotter gaped at the twelve inches of bare thigh revealed by her tight red miniskirt.

Interesting, Jamie thought. *Very interesting.*

He wondered if Love Bytes had a category for this kind of thing.

"You got the hots for Yvette?" he murmured, now bartender-to-customer friendly.

Cotter's expression was wolfish. "Yvette," he said, practically licking his lips. "A perfect name for such an enchanting French pastry."

"Save the lines for her, buddy."

"And would this lovely mademoiselle be available?" Cotter murmured.

Jamie grinned. "She would." He paused. "Care for an introduction?"

Cotter took out a billfold, paid for his coffee and stepped off the barstool, tall and dignified. "I believe I can handle the situation," he said and turned on the savoir faire as he made his way to Yvette's table.

Yvette looked up from applying fresh red lipstick. Her eyes popped as they took in the handsome, expensively tailored professor. She sat up straight, pointing her best assets, and fluffed her hair. "Hi," she said, greeting Cotter with a giggle and a flirtatious flutter of her lashes.

Jamie watched the encounter for a moment, then went into the kitchen, shaking his head. Better luck next time, Love Bytes, he thought. The Big Numero Uno has just toppled off his pedestal.

And Jamie hadn't even had to push very hard.

KATE CAME TO HER SENSES one second before pushing the button that would start Love Bytes on its calculations of the new rankings. She shut off the computer instead, realizing she didn't *want* to see #35JF's numbers plummet. She also realized that she was being a hypocrite. Although she'd prided herself on her scientific objectivity, she'd apparently lost all sense of fair play when it came to Jamie. Perhaps because, for once, her emotions were more deeply involved than her brain.

The right thing to do was to first give him a chance to explain.

So she took a long shower to clear her head and ate a bland lunch to settle her stomach. She found her purse, her car keys, her daring. Although it was going against all her learned instincts of ladylike behavior to force a confrontation, that was what she intended to do. She'd stayed meek and patient one other time, and the result had been another date with Cotter—at Huckleberries.

It was only a short drive to the bar and grill, but once she'd arrived, Kate didn't move from her car for another ten minutes. She sat staring at the weathered shingles and the closed double doors that had been painted the color of huckleberries in the sunshine. Finally, she glanced up to a pair of small windows on the second floor. Jamie's apartment.

She couldn't just barge in on him.

Then again, *why not?*

The interior of Huckleberries was dark and slumberous in the August heat, with only a few desultory customers scattered among the tables. Whistler was lounging at the bar, paging through a copy of the *Mother Earth News*. "Jamie's upstairs," he said with a yawn. "Go on up if y'want."

Kate found the door labeled Private and trudged up the staircase behind it. The door at the top was open, but she knocked anyway, clearing her throat and calling, "Anyone home?" She nudged the door wider and stepped inside. "It's Kate."

The room was big, square, clean but nondescript. There was a computer on a desk in the corner, a pillow and tousled blanket on the couch. She walked over and touched a dent in the pillow made by someone's head.

Voices murmured at the back of the apartment. Kate walked to the connecting hallway. "Yoo-hoo?" she tried. "Hello?"

"Stay in bed, then, woman," Jamie said as he stepped out of one of the bedrooms. "Nothing new there."

Kate's mouth dropped open. Woman? In bed? Now *that* sounded incriminating!

"Kate," Jamie said. "Well, hi."

"I'm sorry," she blurted. "I shouldn't have come."

He restrained her when she started to turn away. "It's okay. I wanted to talk to you—"

She shook his hand off. "Oh, I'm sure. But it was just too difficult to drag yourself away from the woman in your bed."

Jamie had the nerve to smile at her. "You're jealous?"

"Of course I'm jealous!"

"Then think how I feel."

Was he referring to Cotter? To Gordon Hodge?

"There is a woman in my bed," he continued. "Her name's Millie."

"Millie!" Kate said, startled almost speechless.

"Yup. She's sleeping off a bender. It was easier to dump her in my bed than take her to the boarding house where she—"

"The reason you left me was to rescue Millie?"

"Yeah."

Kate blinked. "Oh." That put a different spin on things.

"See, I was downstairs in your kitchen sneaking another piece of cake when the phone rang. I picked up when I recognized Manny's voice on the answering machine. He'd seen Millie and Cecil at the park with a bottle and thought they might get into trouble on their own, so . . ."

"So you took responsibility," Kate said slowly. Did he treat all the patrons of his bar so well?

He shrugged. "I had to. There's no one else who—"

Suzannah came out of the kitchen with a tray. "I made Grandma some tea and toast," she said. "Uh, hi, Ms. Mallory."

"Hi." Kate was having trouble thinking of the proper things to say, but you couldn't go wrong with *hi*.

The bedroom door opened and Millie shambled into the hallway, wrapped in a worn chenille robe, her waist-length gray hair loose and tangled. "Me-oh-my, don't I feel like something the cat dragged in." She blinked, making an effort to prop open her bleary eyelids. "Hi, Carrottop. We havin' a party?"

"No party, Millie," Jamie said, sounding exhausted and impatient. "Just the usual morning-after upheaval."

"Will you try a cup of tea now, Grandma?" Suzannah asked.

Kate was truly speechless as the truth slapped her in the face.

Millie was Jamie's mother.

10

"WELL, OF COURSE I'm Jamie's mother," Millie said a few minutes later when Kate had expressed her surprise. They were sitting at the kitchen table. Millie slung one arm around her son's shoulders. "Wheredja think m'boy got his red hair?"

"Your hair is . . . gray," said Kate. Did she sound as dumb as she felt?

Now that she thought about it, there'd been plenty of clues that Jamie's mother and Millie were the same person. Kate just hadn't picked up on them, which made her wonder why. Was she embarrassed by Millie's behavior? Was it that she hadn't wanted to uncover any more reasons for Jamie's Love Bytes score to sink? Or maybe she simply hadn't looked deep enough, *again*.

If so, she was one heck of a slow learner.

"Jeez, you're right," Millie said, holding out a long gray strand. "I'm so young at heart, I keep forgettin' that I've become an old lady." She sampled a bite of toast. "I think I can eat now, Suze, honey."

Suzannah bounced to her feet. "Eggs, Gran?"

"Scrambled. I sure ain't up to staring a fried egg in the yolk. Haw!"

Suzannah cracked eggs into a mixing bowl. "Dad? Ms. Mallory? Would you like some, too?"

"I've eaten," they said at the same time. Kate smiled and added, "Thanks anyway."

"Jinx," Suzannah said with a giggle.

"Then someone owes me a Coke." Millie started to haul herself out of the chair.

"I'll get it, Gran." Suzannah dashed over and swung open the refrigerator door. She took out milk, butter and the can of cola.

Millie squinted at it as she carefully popped the tab. "If I can't have hair of the dog . . ." she said, saluting Jamie and Kate with the can before she took a swig. "Aw, don't be looking at me like that, Huck. A girl's gotta celebrate her engagement in style."

Jamie snorted. "You call getting falling-down blotto 'in style?'"

Millie shrugged. "What can I say? I'm the life of the party by night and death warmed over, come morning."

Kate felt out of place, as if she shouldn't be participating in this moment of family intimacy. In her parents' house, such obvious digressions, such as Great Aunt Flora's third divorce, were only whispered about or, preferably, swept under the rug. Certainly they were not discussed at the kitchen table.

Her chair scraped across the linoleum as she started to rise. "I have to be going—"

"Hold on there, carrots." Millie snagged Kate's arm. "Me and Suze are shopping for wedding finery after lunch. Why don't you come along? We both could use the fashion advice of a conservative lady schoolteacher like you." She shot a teasing look at Jamie. "Can't be outta style at my own wedding."

"I don't know . . ." Kate said slowly.

Jamie was watching her with a speculative gleam in his eye. "I dare you," he said, and grinned with mischief.

Kate tipped up her chin. "All right, then. I'll go."

Suzannah and Millie exchanged their own mischievous grins. Apparently it was a family trait.

ONE WEEK LATER, the wedding was held at Huckleberries. As was the reception.

Standing among the bar regulars as the justice of the peace performed the ceremony, Kate was musing that the location was strange but an oddly fitting choice. A pair like Millie and Cecil could hardly choose to marry elsewhere.

Still, Kate was having a difficult time understanding Jamie's choice. Owning a bar when your mother is an alcoholic seemed inappropriate. Serving her drinks was definitely wrong, even though, as Jamie had pointed out, she'd get it somewhere if she really wanted to, and he did refuse her everything but beer. On the occasions that Millie had a taste for hard liquor and nothing he said could stop her, his mother went elsewhere.

Big deal, thought Kate, even as she remembered how Jamie was perpetually on call when it came to picking up the pieces. And probably had been since childhood—if such a life could be called childhood. So, okay, maybe he'd chosen the bar because it was all he knew, but, still . . .

At least Millie had been sober all week. She looked suitably bridal in the simple powder blue linen sundress they'd bought on the shopping expedition; she was holding a bouquet of blue salvia, Queen Anne's lace and delphiniums. Suzannah had threaded baby's breath through her grandmother's long gray braid.

Millie's "I do" was clear and crisp, followed by a nudge at Cecil with her elbow and a raucous, "Haw! Haw! Haw!" The wedding guests laughed with her, then applauded as the couple were pronounced husband and wife.

"Let the party begin," Millie announced without delay, picking up the hem of her skirt with one hand and grabbing Cecil with the other.

Suzannah was the maid of honor in a blue chiffon dress with a bustier-style black lace bodice. Jamie had promised her any dress she liked, and not even the presence of a prim schoolteacher could control a headstrong teenager with a credit card. She ran over to the jukebox and pumped it full of quarters. The newlyweds danced their first dance to honky-tonk.

Jamie escorted Suzannah onto the floor. They were followed by Whistler and Charity, then Roger and Rex were dragged out to dance by their seldom seen wives. Soon most of the guests were bopping to the beat.

Taking that as a clue, Kate figured that Millie wasn't going to bother with a receiving line. Likewise, she hoped that the tradition of throwing the bouquet would also be forgotten. She surely didn't want to add another to her collection.

Then again, perhaps this was one time she *needed* to catch the bouquet. The Love Bytes project was drawing to a close; soon she'd select which subject was to be her husband. And since she hadn't thought about how she was going to convince the chosen one to comply, the fate, luck, tradition, old wives' tale, magic—whatever!—of one more bouquet couldn't hurt.

Kate turned around and almost bumped into Gordon Hodge. "Why, Gordon, how are you?" she asked with a smile. "I haven't seen you around lately."

He passed his palm over his brush cut. Kate noticed that it was not in its usual trim, but was ragged around the edges and long on top. "Oh, hiya, Kate." He grinned sheepishly and explained, "I've been so immersed in work I haven't had time to call you."

Kate searched her mind for the name of his employer. "So all's well at Magnatech?" She didn't particularly care, but Love Bytes would want to know—especially since she and Gordon were at three dates and holding.

"I'm sure it is," Gordon said, "but I'm no longer working there. Punch?"

Kate was poleaxed. "Excuse me?"

"Would you like a glass of punch?" Gordon ladled red punch into one of the crystal cups and passed it to Kate.

"Did I hear you correctly? You quit your job at Magnatech?" Kate and Love Bytes were *both* interested in this answer; the stability of Gordon's career had earned him his highest score.

"Actually, I took a leave of absence, but if my patent comes through on the foot massagers I won't be going back." Gordon seemed very pleased with himself. "Someday I'll be as rich and respected as Herbert Smeets."

"B-b-but ..." Kate sputtered.

"Leaving Magnatech was the smartest thing I ever did. I've been swamped with brainstorms ever since, and I can spend night and day in my lab, working on them without interference. At the moment I'm developing a revolutionary style of—" he lowered his voice to a whisper "—toenail clippers. Computerized for the twenty-first century. I'd tell you more, but—" He broke off and looked in all directions, even under the booth where the punch bowl had been set up. "Industrial espionage, you know," he explained at Kate's mystified expression.

"Ah." Kate tried to smile. "I must say I'm shocked, Gordon. You seemed so ... reliable."

"No guts, no glory, as they say."

"Do they?" That sounded more like Jamie than Gordon. Kate frowned. "What about 'slow and steady wins the race'?"

"That's how I used to think." Gordon put down his punch cup. "Now my brain is clicking like a foot-care magnate's should. *Vive la* chiropody!" He disappeared into the crowd.

Dazed and confused, Kate wandered over to the bar, where Manny was dispensing free drinks. "Hiya, Kate," he said. "White wine spritzer?"

"No thanks, Manny. Would you happen to have any margaritas back there?" *Why not?* If Gordon Hodge could kick off the traces and run wild, so could she.

"Won't take but a second to whip one up."

Kate sat on "her" barstool and twirled it around so she could watch the party. Millie and Cecil were doing a half-crocked version of the flamenco to a Spanish Linda Ronstadt tune. Petals flew off Millie's bouquet every time she clapped her hands and stomped her feet. Kate winced, then realized what she was doing.

She was coveting Millie's bridal bouquet!

Although there was no reason for it, Kate felt certain that today's bouquet was meant for her, and, darn it, she'd give back all previous catches if that would guarantee Millie tossing this one her way.

Sweet heaven, she thought, *Get a hold of yourself. Think rational. Sensible. Logical.*

She tried mightily, but it was difficult, if not impossible. Her infatuation with Jamie was growing deeper by the day. Okay, okay, her *love*.

Why had she ever admitted to love? It made their relationship that much tougher to deny—and deny it was something she simply had to do. All her work on Love Bytes was at stake, and her entire hypothesis about choosing the right mate. It was a case of infatuation vs. intelligence. Love versus logic.

She could not give in to sentiment at this late date in the experiment.

Could she?

Fortunately she didn't have to answer that question today. She took a deep breath, crossed her legs and smoothed her slim, slit skirt over her thigh. She wondered if Jamie would notice her new dress. Millie and Suzannah had ganged up to convince Kate to splurge on a tailored, form-fitting, sleeveless dress, several inches shorter and quite a bit more revealing than the styles she usually wore. It had a low-cut sweetheart neckline and was red to boot—a deep subtly sexy wine red.

Kate knew she'd never be like Yvette, the sexy blonde who was wiggling around the dance floor in a peekaboo lace blouse and tight satin hot pants. Not that she wanted to be, either. When Jamie had made her really look at herself in that mirror, she'd seen that she wasn't necessarily his image of a perfect partner and for sure she wasn't completely her parents' studious scientist daughter. She was simply the Katrina Mallory she, herself, wanted to be, even if she wasn't yet sure what all that entailed. The red dress was a first step in the discovery process.

Manny placed a frosty glass on the bar. "Here you go, Kate. One margarita, built to please."

Kate took a sip and smiled her thanks. "Very nice, Manny," she said, hiding her disappointment. The drink was just a regular margarita, not strawberry, and it didn't taste nearly as good as the one Jamie had served her. It lacked a certain . . . magic.

Snapping her fingers overhead, Yvette coochie-cooed up to the bar. "I'll have a Pink Squirrel, Manny, sugar. Hiya, Kate. Didja see my new guy? Isn't he gorgeous? And real smart, too—he even belongs to an exclusive club that only lets in men with high IQs."

"Mensa?" Kate guessed. Her parents were members, but Kate had never wanted to join.

Yvette nodded happily. "The Folger twins are so jealous—it's great."

"Wonderful," agreed Kate, with more feeling. When hanging out at Huckleberries she'd noticed that Yvette would gladly have taken Jamie off her hands. In case it turned out that Love Bytes *forced* her to choose Jamie, it couldn't hurt to eliminate the competition.

"He drives a Corvette, isn't that a hoot? Yvette, Corvette—get it?" The blonde giggled. "And he's a professor, if you can believe that!"

"A professor," Kate repeated. Didn't Cotter drive a Corvette?

"There he is," Yvette squealed. "Honeybuns—over here!"

Even though Cotter had never expressed a predilection for buxom blondes, Kate was not surprised to see him emerge from the crowded dance floor. However, *he* was surprised to see *her.*

Cotter sat on the next stool over; immediately Yvette snuggled up to his side, cooing in his ear. "Good afternoon, Katrina," he said with straight-faced propriety, even though Kate had noticed that he'd given Yvette's derriere a little squeeze.

"An interesting wedding, wasn't it?" Kate said. "I hadn't realized you were acquainted with the newlyweds." Pleased to make Cotter squirm, she smiled a smile that looked innocent but was wicked in intent. Millie and Cecil were the type of people Cotter considered riffraff. But then, so was Yvette.

"I'm not," he answered, with a wary glance at Millie, who was now doing the cha-cha.

"He's my date," said Yvette. "Kiss-kiss." She twined her arm around Cotter's neck and planted a juicy kiss on his cheek.

Cotter took a pressed linen square from his pocket and scrubbed at the smear of red lipstick. "Yvette, sweetheart, would you please give me a moment alone with Katrina?"

Kate shook her head. "Oh, that's not necess—"

"Anything you want, honeybuns. I'll go to the powder room to repair my lipstick." Yvette shook her finger at Kate. "But I won't be long. You be sure to keep your hands off my fella."

"I'll try," Kate said dryly. Yvette took her Pink Squirrel with her.

Cotter asked Manny for a double of whatever was closest at hand. Kate wondered if Jamie had ever "done him." As of today, she was figuring Cotter for something stiff and expensive—with a Wild Turkey chaser.

Cotter's forehead furrowed; his eyes were dark with apology and sympathy for her plight. "I'm so sorry, Katrina."

"Sorry?" she trilled. How could Cotter be sorry for her? *She* had Jamie! "Whatever for?"

"Well, you know—Yvette." He wagged his head with apology. "I should have told you."

"Told me what? Are you doing something—" Kate lowered her voice "—naughty? Something to be ashamed of?"

Cotter's color rose as he stammered, "I—I—uh—"

She relaxed against the bar. "Aw, what the heck, Cotter. Who cares? We only dated, and not even exclusively."

"That's true. You had your own little frolic among the riffraff, didn't you, Katrina? With that unconventional bartender who's named after a fruit."

Kate straightened, her eyes flashing with anger. "For one thing, I do not frolic—"

"Certainly not with me." Cotter sniffed.

"Thank heaven," she snapped.

He turned mealymouthed. "I'm sorry if you entertained certain expectations, Katrina, but the fact is you're simply not my, uh, type—" He broke off to stare at her dress. "*However*, you are looking quite—"

"Forget it, Cotter. You're too late." And about a million points short.

"Mmm, are you sure, dear Katrina?" His voice was oily with insinuation. "Once I've worked the attraction to Yvette out of my system, perhaps we can try again . . . ?"

For the moment unaware that she'd once felt the same way about her relationship with Jamie, Kate rolled her eyes. Sure, like she'd want a man who actually operated under the double standard of the good girl, bad girl system!

So #27CC was another subject she'd badly misjudged, and, golly gee, the Love Bytes candidates were dropping left and right, weren't they? It was more and more likely that Jamie would end up being her only truly eligible prospect. Kate's heart leapt. Wouldn't that be a hoot?

She fixed Cotter with a steely stare. "It'll never happen, Professor. You and I have no claims on each other," she responded, blithely ignoring the pages of Love Bytes data that said she was lying through her teeth. "Not now, not in the future. You're free to do as you please. But it would be nice if you'd treat Yvette with a little respect. Let her down gently, okay?"

Cotter stood and fussily straightened his ultraexpensive, subdued silk tie. "Is that how you did it with your bartender?"

Kate blanched. "I haven't let him down."

"But eventually you shall."

"I won't," Kate vowed, more to herself than to the departing professor.

Somehow, no matter what developed with Love Bytes, she would find a way not to let Jamie down. And as for respect . . .

That was something she still owed him.

JAMIE FINALLY CAUGHT UP with Kate at the buffet tables. She was holding a thin wooden skewer, trying to choose between smoked turkey and chilled shrimp.

"Take both," he suggested.

She speared the succulent turkey. "My zipper may split."

Jamie glanced down at her form-fitting dress. "Hmm, look at that. There's a redhead's dress if I ever saw one," he purred. His fingertips brushed past her waist and lingered at the flare of her hip. "You may be right. I don't think you can squeeze another bite into it."

"But that's not where I'm putting it," Kate sassed. She popped the slice of turkey into her mouth. "Yummy."

"Yummy," Jamie hummed into her ear, and he wasn't talking about the spread. "Have you tried the desserts?" he asked, nudging her along the line of tables. "I'd love to watch you lick whipped cream off—"

"Jamie, really. You seem to be forgetting that this is a wedding reception, not a pickup line. Behave yourself."

"Seeing as how the bride isn't concerning herself with proper behavior, I don't see why I should be."

Kate glanced over her shoulder. The newlyweds were rollicking around the dance floor to "The Beer Barrel Polka." Millie still looked peppy, but Cecil was drooping badly. "Your mother seems to have an impressive dance repertoire at her disposal."

"There's not a lot else to do in bars. She also plays a mean game of darts."

"And do you?"

Jamie didn't care for the hint of what he took as pity for his misbegotten childhood. He didn't want Kate's pity. "I learned to play the piano, remember?"

"And to name the drink that distills the essence of a stranger's soul." Kate tilted her head to one side. "Tell me, Jamie, if *you* were a drink, what drink would you be?"

He laughed. No one had ever thought to ask him that question before. "Oh, probably a cheap draft beer," he said casually.

Kate shook her head. "No. I see you more as a glass of Bordeaux. A rich red, tart, amusing, piquant, but with a deep, smoky, satisfying undertone."

"Hmm, not half bad, Kate." He handed her a glass of the ersatz champagne. "Maybe you've got the talent yourself."

"Only when it comes to you, Jamie. But was I right? Are you more than meets the eye?"

He was still trying to keep the conversation lighthearted. "Isn't everyone?"

"Some more than others, it seems. Who would have thought Gordon would turn into a crazy inventor and Cotter into a hound."

"Been talking to your boyfriends, have you?"

"No."

"No?"

"They're not my boyfriends, I mean."

Jamie looked at her, studying the prim line of her lips and the unbidden sparkle of her emerald eyes. That was Kate—some of this, some of that—enough of a mystery that he could spend the rest of his life uncovering her secrets.

By denying her interest in Gordon and Cotter, and meaning it, Kate was revealing more than she realized. Jamie felt renewed hope. It was a rush, making him want to dance and shout, making him believe that no dream was beyond his reach. Starting with Kate.

"Care to dance?" he asked, sweeping away her champagne before she'd tasted it. She hung back until he took her hand and coaxed her. "Aw, c'mon, Katy, dance with me."

She came to him reluctantly. "I don't know how to polka. I'll stumble all over myself and look like a fool in front of your friends."

"They're your friends, too, and so what if you can't polka? I don't know how to waltz. We can compromise."

Which was why, as the other guests did a wild, gal-lumphing polka around them, Jamie and Kate danced cheek-to-cheek.

LATER THEY SHARED a piece of wedding cake. The party had quieted as the lights were turned down. A soft country bal-lad wafted from the jukebox and candles flickered at the booths occupied by foot-weary guests. Millie had set a mean pace that had worn most of them out.

Kate ate a tiny spun-sugar rose off the tines of her fork. "Would it be fair to say that you must be relieved to have your mother safely married?"

Jamie was slumped against the back of the booth, his shirtsleeves rolled up, his tie askew. She'd discovered that he chose ties that were as goofy as his boxer shorts; this one was silk-screened with a scene from *Father of the Bride.*

"Six of one, half a dozen of the other," he said. "I may end up watching over Cecil, in addition to Millie." He shrugged. "Maybe not."

"Is Cecil an alcoholic?"

"I couldn't say, but I don't think so. He doesn't usually go overboard, except when Millie's on a bad streak. He's weak, can't say no to her."

Kate glanced across the room to where Millie and Cecil were slow-dancing under the canopy of twinkling Christ-mas tree lights hung from the rafters. Mrs. Apthorpe looked to be supporting Mr. Apthorpe, whose powder blue tux and ruffled shirt were by now hopelessly wrinkled.

"Cecil's an odd chap," Kate commented. "Is it true that his father is an earl and Cecil's the black sheep of the Ap-thorpe family, exiled to the United States?"

Jamie still had the energy to laugh. "That's what Cecil would like you to believe."

"It's not true?"

He leaned forward. "Cecil is originally from Milwaukee. He had a few bit parts in Hollywood back in the forties and toured with the road show of *A Chorus Line* in the seventies as a lighting technician. Now all the world's his stage."

Kate chuckled. "And to think I believed his story about riding bareback in Scotland with Princess Margaret."

"By next year Cecil will probably have assumed another identity. Before this, he was a diamond miner from South Africa."

"Does Millie know?"

Jamie snorted. "Cecil's just what Millie ordered. She doesn't have what you'd call a long attention span. Or staying power."

Kate nibbled on another bite of cake, mulling over Jamie's position. His family situation wasn't ideal, as far as Love Bytes went, but he should earn extra points for being such a dedicated, caring son, now that she knew the truth.

"You always call her Millie," she said. "I think that's why I got confused."

"Millie's not a Mom type."

Kate's brow furrowed. "I feel so bad for—"

Jamie made a slicing motion with his hand. "Don't pity me, Kate."

She froze, stunned by his sudden ferocity. After a long moment she bowed her head, resting her hands palms up on the table. "I was going to say I feel bad for Suzannah, not having her mother, making tea and toast for her grandmother instead of the other way around...."

"She has Charity. Charity makes up for—" He broke off, shaking his head as he dropped his hands over hers. "I'm sorry for snapping at you, Kate. I'm a jerk."

She smiled as their fingers intertwined. "No, Jamie, you're wonderful, incredibly generous and responsible. Much more so than I expected."

"Then I hate to think what you expected."

Kate could have bitten her tongue. Why was it so difficult for her to find the right words to tell Jamie how she felt about him?

Maybe because she was continually torn in two directions.

Infatuation versus intellect. Love versus logic.

Or maybe because she was making complicated what was actually simple. All she had to say was *I love you—*

"Time to throw the bouquet!" trumpeted Millie. "All you single gals gather 'round, the desperate ones down front— haw!"

The group formed near the bar. Yvette scurried by, tottering on high heels.

Kate wasn't paying attention. She was still holding Jamie's hands, looking into his eyes, trying to figure out how she could follow her heart and yet not abandon her brain.

"Ms. Mallory, c'mon," said Suzannah as she passed the booth. "Don't you want to catch the bouquet?"

Jamie squeezed her hands. "Kate?"

She came back to her senses and looked at the knot of women in their best dresses, young and old faces glowing with excitement, clapping, laughing, extending their hands toward Millie as she held up the bedraggled bouquet. "Oh!" Kate said. "The bouquet—!"

She swung her legs around, black heels first, and slid from the booth, calling, "Wait for me, Millie."

Suzannah made a beckoning motion. "Hurry up. She's going to throw it."

"I'm coming!" Kate stood, took a second to yank her tight dress down over her thighs, and tried to look dignified as

her heels tap-tap-tapped double time, her long legs stretching to propel her across the dance floor.

Millie had climbed up on the bar. She whipped her braid
over her shoulder and held the bouquet out teasingly.
"One," she said, winding up.

"Two," the guests chimed in. Millie's arm swung forward.

Kate had reached the back of the group. Forgetting any
notion of etiquette, she elbowed her way toward the front,
her hands reaching . . .

"Three!" The bouquet made a graceful arc through the
air, blue and white ribbons fluttering in its wake.

It swooped toward Kate and Yvette. Kate, the taller of the
pair, leaped up and snatched the bouquet away an instant
before Yvette's long red fingernails could snag it. When she
landed, Kate skidded on the smear where Millie and Cecil
had dropped hunks of wedding cake while they were feed-
ing each other. Her feet slipped out from beneath her.

She yelped as she went down, her legs splitting in either
direction. Her dress tore upward from the side slit, the gar-
net-and-silver necklace flew up into her face and an inch-
wide run raced through one of her delicate silk stockings
from heel to knee.

The bouquet popped out of her hands.

Yvette made a grab for it, but Kate's instincts were firing
on full alert even through her rising embarrassment. She
threw herself forward and landed on the bouquet in an un-
dignified sprawl.

The guests cheered and catcalled as Kate slowly picked
herself and the crushed bouquet up off the floor, her face
flaming with color beneath the necklace looping off her
ears. She was a mess—hair tousled, one heel broken off, the
run in her stocking still running as it disappeared beneath
her ripped skirt. And she was mortified, utterly mortified.

But she had the bouquet!

Jamie appeared out of the crowd and swept Kate up in his arms. Throwing his head back with laughter, he twirled, spinning Kate around in circles until she was giddy with motion, clutching the bouquet to her breast, laughing and hiccuping and gasping, not even caring that she'd just destroyed forever her reputation as a sedate schoolteacher.

11

THE AIR WAS BLUE with dusk by the time the party had officially broken up and Jamie drove Kate back to her house in his Jeep. After he'd pulled up to the curb and shut off the ignition, silence fell between them. Kate fingered the blue and white flowers in her lap.

Déjà vu. Only three or so months ago she'd done the same thing with Rodney Pfaeffle. The irony of the situation was not lost on her.

"I did this," she found herself confessing.

"What?"

"Three months ago I was returning from another wedding after catching the bouquet. The guy I was with was just, well, *awful*—" there simply wasn't another word for poor Rod "—and I wasn't in a great mood about it, seeing as how I knew maybe a dozen single men, but none of them seemed..." She wanted to say *magical* but instead she took a deep breath and said, "Viable."

"Viable?"

"As prospective husbands." If this story didn't scare Jamie away for good, nothing would.

"Aha," he said. "I see ..."

He did? He couldn't.

"Are the prospects better this time around?" he asked.

"I'm not sure." She was afraid to look at him. "Well, that's not entirely true. You're certainly a much nicer escort than Rodney Pfaeffle."

Jamie got out of the Jeep, crossed to her side and opened the door. Kate swung her legs around, but didn't slide out. "I hope I haven't ruined things between us by speaking so bluntly," she murmured. "I know how it is with you."

"Then maybe you should clue me in."

Kate closed her eyes. She was wading in deeper and deeper and deeper. Soon there'd be no getting out. "Charity let me know that you're not a marrying man."

"Now, why would she say that? I married her daughter, didn't I?"

She peeped up at Jamie. He didn't look spooked . . . yet. "But you've resisted remarrying for ten years now. That's a long time. Bachelors tend to guard their freedom, whereas society expects women to desire marriage before all else. Of course, then you have to throw in the process of natural selection, and the hormones that inspire feelings of—"

"Hey, teach?" Jamie interrupted.

"Yes?"

"Thanks for the lecture and everything," he said, "but has it ever occurred to you that Charity might've been wrong? That the reason I haven't remarried has nothing to do with being a swinging single, and everything to do with the fact that I was waiting for the right woman?"

"There's also the biological imperative of—of—" She faltered to a stop, then whispered, "What did you say?"

Standing in the open door, Jamie put his arms around her waist. The bouquet rustled between them. "Your brain might be all clotted up with science, but you're still the most exciting woman I've ever known, Kate Mallory. You stir up things inside me, things that I'd forgotten I wanted. You challenge me to be a better person."

Kate put her hand up to his cheek, feeling the fine rasp of his beard against her palm. "Jamie, you don't have to be a better person. You're fine the way you are."

She'd spoken instinctively, but an immediate question popped into her head. Was she lying to him? Didn't all the numbers, equations and rankings of Love Bytes add up to just one thing: *That he might be good, but not good enough.*

If she could have done it at that very moment, Kate would have smashed her computer to pieces and torn the Love Bytes printout into tiny shreds.

Because it seemed obvious. Jamie was everything she wanted in a man.

Words were streaming out of him. "There are so many things I want to do. Take some business courses at the college, maybe, and learn the best methods to run the bar efficiently. I might study music, even. Learn how to really play the piano. Huckleberries could use some live entertainment. I'd like to build a house with my own two hands, the way Whistler and Charity did. And I always wanted to learn to sail. Being on the water was the only thing I liked about the marines."

Kate's mouth was hanging open, her hands locked at the back of his neck. "I didn't know you were in the marines."

He laughed shortly. "Surprise. I joined when I was eighteen, only stayed in for a few years before I married Sunny. I thought the discipline would do me some good, but, no surprise, that was also what I hated about it."

Kate's laugh was amazed. "Somehow, I can't see you in the marines."

"There're lots of things you can't see about me."

She sobered. "You're right."

"But I'd be glad to show you." He leaned into the Jeep, bringing his face down to hers. "One warning, though. It might take years."

Kate couldn't breathe. She couldn't speak. She could only nod.

And kiss him back when he kissed her, his lips warm and his tongue gentle, his hands stroking in circles of gentle sensation over her back. Her heart felt as if it was ready to burst, but still there were the doubts with which she'd struggled all along.

"Oh, Jamie, I don't know. I'm just so scared that—" Tongue-tied, she shook her head.

"What scares you?" he urged.

"Making the wrong choice." She dropped her forehead against his shoulder and blew out a ragged breath.

"Is making a mistake so terrible?" Jamie murmured. "How would a person get anywhere if they didn't take risks?"

"Good question, I guess, but scientists don't take risks. They prepare and they do research. They check and double-check and do double blinds and quality control. Everything is calculated down to the nth degree. No risk. No surprise." *No allowances for magic.*

"Maybe that's so, Kate, but you're not a scientist."

"Well, a science teacher, anyway. I use the methods in my classes. And I think I am one at heart."

He shook his head. "Uh-uh."

"Oh, what do you know, Jamie," she scoffed. Inside, she was confused. If she wasn't a scientist like her parents, then what was she? Who was the person reflected in the mirror?

Softly Jamie said, "You're a woman, Katy."

Her eyes widened. "I'm a science teacher," she insisted.

"First, you're a woman."

She thought of herself on the kitchen countertop, openly naked and wanting, of the persistent longing for a family that had been the undefined and unspoken reason behind Love Bytes, and had to agree with a tentative nod.

"Told ya so," he teased.

"Oh, Jamie." She yearned to forget everything but the pleasure of being held in his arms. His pull was so strong she actually felt like a magnet attracted to steel. The old "opposites attract" theory, she thought, clinging to her pragmatism. The sizzling connection of polar opposites, the mind-drugging effects of infatuation. Yes, it was possible to explain away her longing for Jamie with proven scientific theories.

Not entirely, said a voice inside. It was her heart, second-guessing her brain.

"The various stages of so-called love have been studied by scientists," she blurted. "Under the influence of infatuation, the brain produces certain chemicals that distort a person's perception of reality, like amphetamines. You and I are in the euphoric stage, and—" She gulped.

"I'm thinking a little science goes a long way," Jamie said to the air.

"Wait," Kate insisted. "See, infatuation—it doesn't last. We'd have four years, max, before the endorphins settled down and then—"

"What?" he interrupted. "*Bam*, we fall out of love just like that?"

She shook her head. "Not exactly. But infatuation would give way to comfort. 'Companionship love,' technically speaking."

"Okay, that might be so. And so what?"

"You don't strike me as a guy who's looking for simple companionship."

Turning his face aside, Jamie stepped back and away. He slammed his hands onto the Jeep's roll bar and held on good and tight. Kate shrank back into the shadowed interior, clutching the silly, disheveled bouquet to her chest. She was looking pretty silly and disheveled herself, but still she'd persisted in spouting her scientific gobbledygook.

The truth burst out of Jamie, searing and blunt. "What you're saying is you think I'd dump you when the sex is no longer so hot."

Kate's voice shook. "I don't mean to . . ."

Jamie ducked his head lower so he could see her face. He needed to gauge her reaction. "Maybe what you really mean is that *you* won't be interested in *me* after the sex isn't as hot."

She gasped. Her face went white, with splotches of pink burning on her cheeks, and he figured he'd hit the nail on the head. According to Love Bytes, he just wasn't the kind of man Kate was looking to marry.

Which made him feel like something she'd scrape off the sole of her shoe.

"That's not true," she cried, then ruined it by adding weakly, "I don't think."

With a low growl of frustration he pushed away from the Jeep and paced along the sidewalk as far as Buntz's seven-foot hedge, then back again. A couple of the small green apples from Kate's tree had dropped over her twig-and-wattle fence; he kicked them into the gutter.

"So, Kate," he said, coming back to lean against the front hood. Folding his arms across his chest, he tried to appear relaxed even though his muscles were tight and his gut was churning with tension. He drew his gaze along the long, lovely line of Kate's legs, still dangling out the side of the Jeep, their grace unmarred by the run in her stocking. "So, Kate," he repeated, looking away again, "tell me, exactly what qualities are you looking for in a husband?"

The flowers quivered as she tightened her fingers. "Please don't—"

"Tell me."

"Fine," she snapped, sliding down until her one intact heel hit the sidewalk. The deepening dusk gave her hair a coppery gleam as she lifted her head to meet his eyes. "Stability."

"I've owned and operated Huckleberries for nine years."

"Honesty."

"Have I ever lied to you?"

She shrugged and said, "Character."

He smiled. "You can't deny I'm a character."

She pressed her lips together. Then after a moment responded, "How about being willing to commit?"

"Commit what? A crime?"

"You see!" she charged, her nose in the air. "You make jokes instead of answering seriously."

"But no one knows until it's lasted how strong a commitment really is," he protested. "All I can say is that I *am* willing to risk it."

Her brows drew together. "You are?"

"Just try me."

She avoided responding by saying scoldingly, "Ethics."

"What does that tone of voice mean?"

"Well, Jamie, it doesn't seem quite ethical to own a bar when your own mother has a problem with drinking. Millie practically lives at Huckleberries. All that exposure to temptation can't be good for her. There was an open bar and even champagne at the wedding."

"Manny was instructed not to serve Cecil and Millie. The champagne was the nonalcoholic kind. Tasted like sour ginger ale."

"Oh. I didn't realize."

"And as for Huckleberries . . ." Jamie came around the open door again and stood before Kate, his eyes engaging hers. "Unlike you, I've known Millie all of my life. I've seen her go in and out of treatment centers, watched her fall off the wagon and get back on and fall off again a month later. I can't control her compulsion to drink, Kate."

"No, but—"

"Suze goes to Al-Anon, and I do, too, on occasion. I made the choice years ago that it was better to have Millie at Huckleberries where I can keep an eye on her than to stand by while she carouses all over town where who knows what trouble she'd get into. If you find that *unethical . . .*" He shrugged. "So be it."

Kate's head drooped. "I'm sorry. I hadn't thought about it like that."

"There's more than one way of looking at things. Such a methodical, objective scientist should know that."

"Yeah," she whispered. "Monica told me that, too."

"Hey, it's not so bad," Jamie said. He took one of her hands, tugged her away from the Jeep and slammed the door. "You simply need to reconsider some of your categories. Like—"

"Did you say *categories?*" Her tone was suspicious.

"Umm, qualities, I meant," he corrected and hurried on before she could think about the slip. "Shouldn't the ideal husband also have a sense of humor?" He didn't remember seeing that in the Love Bytes printout.

"Ye-e-es," she said, drawing the word out, still leery. "I guess I hadn't thought of that, but it's true that humor is important to a lasting marriage. Sometimes I hear Monica and Ed laughing all the way over at my house."

"And there's just plain caring." Did Kate actually care for Cotter and Gordon and all the rest, or did she only admire certain qualities in them? "I think you know how I feel about you."

"And I care for you, too, Jamie. You know I do."

He caught her around the waist and backed her up against the twig gate. "Better watch your words, there, Katy. I thought I heard you say 'I do.'"

She smiled with shy beauty and tapped the flowers against his chest. "Maybe you should tell me what qualities you're looking for." She hesitated, giving a small squirm beneath his hands. "In a wife."

He loved the way her eyes skated briefly across his face, grave but reverent, almost as if she admired him as much as the paragons of Love Bytes, and then averted bashfully for a moment before the thick lashes lifted, slowly, slowly, as though his own desires were dragging her gaze back up to meet his.

"I want three things," he said softly.

Her lips parted. "Yes?"

He couldn't resist pressing a gentle kiss on her mouth. "I want a woman with hair the color of sunrise."

She withdrew slightly, brushing at her feathery bangs, tucking some of her hair behind her ear.

Swallowing the ache that was growing inside him, Jamie stared into Kate's eyes and realized the exact definition of what he'd been craving from her. "I want a woman who has as much love and respect for me as I do for her."

She closed her eyes and nodded silently. A neighbor's door opened and closed, letting out a burst of canned sit-com laughter from a blaring television.

Jamie drew a deep breath. "And I want a woman who wants to marry me so badly she's willing to throw herself on top of a bunch of flowers to guarantee it."

Kate made a choking sound and wound her arms around his shoulders. "I'm never going to live that one down, am I?" she said, half in humor, half in horror, and was suddenly kissing him with a deep, urgent desire. She opened her mouth, pressing even closer; her breasts moved against his chest.

"Katy," he whispered. He cupped her head, holding it still as he covered her mouth with his and applied himself to the task of driving her out of her relentlessly scientific mind with kisses that came so fast they ran into one long, liquid melding of heat and hunger and need.

Kate's mouth slid against his. "Can you come—"

"*Yes.*"

"Inside? The house," she panted.

He sucked at her bottom lip. "Preferably."

For a moment he thought that Kate was making the snuffling sounds he heard as she nuzzled her nose along the line of his jaw and up to his ear, her darting tongue exquisitely adept. She did groan.

But not growl. Jamie looked down an instant before Boris launched himself at his leg.

"Bad dog!" screeched Kate.

Jamie leapt two feet backward into the gutter. Boris's bared teeth snapped at air as he landed on the sidewalk, paws splayed, short tail uncurled and erect. Jamie yelled, "Gate, Kate!" as the ill-mannered boxer scrambled around with a growl.

Jamie pivoted and dived through the open passenger-side window, into the safety of the Jeep. The dog's bulky body battered at the barrier between them, his toenails scratching on metal as he slobbered over the door handle.

Jamie tipped himself upright and peeked out. Kate was safely inside the gate, watching Boris and biting her lip. The boxer gave up on assaulting the Jeep and lunged at Kate's bouquet, which she'd dropped on the sidewalk. Growling, he flipped it up and caught it between his teeth.

"I hope this doesn't mean bad luck," Kate said with a shaky laugh as Boris tore at the bouquet, scattering the blue petals of the delphiniums with a vicious shake of his head.

Jamie hung his head out the window. "We're going to make our own luck, Kate," he promised.

She smiled through the darkness. "Not while you're over there and I'm in here." Boris's ears stiffened as he lifted his head, mangled stems poking out from under his jowls. "I could call for Mr. Buntz."

Reluctantly Jamie shook his head. "I should really be getting back to Huckleberries, anyway. There's a big mess, lots to do...."

Kate's disappointment was as clear as day. "Sure, I understand."

"Besides, you have a decision to make." He turned the ignition key and the Jeep's engine fired, drawing a low growl of warning from Boris.

"I do?" Kate's voice was soft, but Jamie still heard it.

He pulled out, made an efficient U-turn and braked again at the curb. Kate was standing at the gate, her hands twined around the scalloped twigs, and he rested both arms on the car door, indulging in a good long look.

Dress ripped up one thigh, pale bare shoulders canted because of the missing heel, Kate made a beautiful wreck. Whatever the outcome of Love Bytes, he was going to have her. And keep her.

"You've got to make up your mind, Katy, darling," he called softly to her through the summer night, "because the next time we make love it's going to be forever."

She stared, the smile slowly fading from her lips.

With a set jaw he put the Jeep in gear and drove away. Although Jamie didn't consider himself a patient man, he was determined to settle for nothing less than true love and it was vital that Kate came to realize the same.

He'd give her a week, tops.

12

"Pregnant!"

"Pregnant," Monica repeated, stunned.

"But how?" came Kate's plaintive cry.

"Seeing as it's all Jamie's fault, you should be able to figure it out."

"That scoundrel," Kate said.

Monica hooted. "Jamie or Boris?"

"Boris, of course." Kate looked away, unable to stop an indulgent smile. "Well, Jamie, too, I suppose." She swiveled away from the computer to face Monica, who was sitting in the rocking chair, fuming. Kate tapped her chin. "When, exactly?"

Monica scowled. "I don't keep track of your love life."

Kate's eyebrows rose.

Monica grinned. "At least, not *that* closely."

"It had to be the Sunday we had dinner on the patio. We were carrying groceries when we came home and I don't remember checking the gate. Jamie might have left it open."

"Just once is all it takes." Although both of their yards were fenced, there was no barrier between them. If Kate's fence was open, so, in effect, was Monica's.

"Bad timing," Kate murmured.

"Yes, well, thanks to Jamie, Boris got into my yard and now poor little Natasha's gonna have the ugliest puppies this town has ever seen. With Boris as the daddy, they're sure to be as mean as sin, too. I'll never find homes for them!" Monica wailed.

"Oh, I don't know. The puppies might turn out okay. See, sometimes with crossbreeding you get lucky and inherit the best qualities of both parents. Look at how certain insular lines of European royalty would arrange the occasional marriage with an outsider to punch up their inbred blood-lines—"

"Are we still talking about puppies?" Monica inter-rupted.

"Of course." Kate flushed. "What else?"

"Hmm. You are something of a princess. And Jamie's sure got punch."

"I was not talking about Jamie and me. Both our blood-lines are untraceable and common as dirt."

"Okay, okay." Monica chuckled. "But I'm still going to be left with a litter of butt-ugly puppies."

"I'll take one. Suzannah might like a puppy."

"So that's two?"

"Uh, I don't know. Maybe only one. It depends."

Monica looked askance. "On if you decide to intermin-gle bloodlines?"

"That's up to Love Bytes." Kate traced her finger along the computer's keyboard.

"Oh, Kate, no," Monica said. "I thought you'd come to your senses about that. You absolutely cannot be serious about letting a computer choose your perfect mate!"

"But all my work . . ." Kate lamented. "The theory be-hind the program is sound."

"I never knew you were so stubborn." Monica rocked back and forth, squinching her eyes at her blockhead of a friend. "Think about it, woman. Could you really go through with marrying Cotter? Gordon Hodge? That li-brarian on the Harley—Kevin something? Or, worst case scenario, *Rodney Pfaeffle?*"

"Rod's name can't possibly come up."

"And the others?"

Kate imagined proposing marriage to Cotter or Gordon or Michael Ianucci, the nice, third-ranked tax attorney whom she hadn't actually dated in several months. The mental picture was absurd, the actual possibility ludicrous. There was only one man she wanted.

Still. Infatuation versus intellect. Love versus logic.

Magic versus matchmaking.

It was a quandary.

"The new school year begins in a few days," Kate said seriously. "I want to have this settled, one way or another."

"Huh. So where's Jamie ranked, anyway?"

"I don't know. I haven't run the current numbers in quite a while."

"Chicken?"

"Probably," Kate admitted, miserable with indecision.

Monica got up and pulled the rocking chair closer to the computer screen. "But you're all set to go? The stats and what-all are up-to-date?"

"Yes."

"So, do it! Aren't you dying of curiosity?" Monica rubbed her hands together. "I know I am."

"I thought you didn't want me to," Kate said, stalling.

"Just 'cause Love Bytes produces a name doesn't mean you actually have to marry the sucker—er, the lucky winner, I mean."

Kate rolled her eyes. "You think this is a game."

Monica chortled. "Heck, yeah!" She punched the Page Down key. "Who's this? Gordon Hodge? Shouldn't he have lower numbers in Style? That pocket protector of his has got to cost him twenty-five points, at least."

Kate cleared the screen. "Not necessarily. Would you rather scrub ink stains out of dress shirts?"

"Hair spray," Monica said. "Or is it a dab of toothpaste? I forget."

"Huh?"

"To remove ink stains. Lordy, Kate, if you're going to get married you'd better start reading Heloise."

"Who is Heloise? Did she write a home economics textbook?"

Monica flapped her hand. "Forget it. Let's get back to Love Bytes. Can I see Jamie's scores?"

"You may not!"

"Aw, shucks. Why not?"

His Sexual Attraction scores, for one, Kate thought. She'd had to recalibrate the scale after their first time together. And again after the second. If her schoolmarm reputation hadn't already been destroyed at the wedding, public consumption of her Physical Response-Female, scores would do it single-handedly. And she could just imagine the kick Monica would get out of Kate's attempts to formulate a definition of the kind of chemical reaction that didn't take place in a test tube.

Kate cleared her throat. "Monica, would you be so kind as to show yourself out?"

"Double shucks." Pouting, Monica got up and shoved the rocker back in place. "You're no fun."

"Love Bytes is serious stuff," Kate murmured, preoccupied with double-checking the numbers she'd plugged in to the equations from the various files. After what she'd learned at Millie's wedding, the rankings of Gordon and Cotter were sure to take a nosedive. Likewise, now that she understood the reasons for Jamie's life-style, and had adjusted some of the categories to shore up the areas she'd neglected, his score was sure to soar. The downgrading she'd done to his numbers when she was in such a snit after waking up without him had been deleted, and she'd even managed to sneak in a few bonus points.

No less than he deserved, and maybe enough to take Jamie all the way up to Number One. Kate crossed her fingers. Monica gave up squinting at the screen, shook her black hair out of her eyes and tiptoed from the room.

"Give Natasha my condolences," Kate murmured distractedly.

"Ha!" Monica said from the hallway. "She's so pleased with herself I'm beginning to wonder if there's more to Boris than meets the eye. Natasha may be looking very impressed, but she's not saying."

Neither was Kate. She mumbled something to herself, the computer screen flashing with numbers as her long fingers skipped over the keys.

JAMIE AND GREGORY GORDON Hodge were also sitting in front of a computer. Gregory Gordon was demonstrating the bookkeeping software and helping Jamie put the Huckleberries accounts on disk.

"So, Gregory Gordon," Jamie said. "You interested in Suze? I saw you dancing with her at the wedding."

Gregory Gordon looked mortified. "S-sorry, sir."

Jamie clapped him on the back. "No need to apologize. I'm a little lovesick, myself, these days."

Gregory Gordon looked stunned.

"As a matter of fact, you could probably help me out with something on the computer concerning my, ah, lady friend. It's not quite legit, but are you game?"

Gregory Gordon looked intrigued. "Sure."

Jamie approached the subject carefully. "You know when you and Suze got into the school's computer system?"

"We've never done it again, Mr. Flynn, I swear."

"I know." Another man might point out that there'd been no need after Suze had received her passing grade and been rewarded with the bonus as promised. Considering what he was going to ask of Gregory Gordon, Jamie couldn't afford to be hypocritical. He pushed his misgivings aside. Good thing he had muscles; guilt weighed a ton.

"What I want you to do is give me the password for Ms. Mallory's private files. The one you used to make the printout." He forced a chuckle. "I'm going to play kind of a joke on her."

Gregory Gordon hesitated.

"It's okay, I swear. We're practically unofficially engaged." *With the emphasis on the unofficially.*

"Then I guess that's all right," Gregory Gordon said. But he showed Jamie how to access Kate's files and made his getaway in record time, stopping only long enough to bestow a lovelorn look on Suzannah as she came up the stairs.

"Hey, Dad, what are you doing with the computer? G.G. looked like he swallowed the mouse."

Jamie sure didn't need Suze poking her freckled nose into Love Bytes. "Go clean your room," he said. He couldn't remember if it was any messier than his own, but the odds were fifty-fifty.

"Sheesh," Suze said, taking a Coke from the fridge. She stomped toward her room, yelling over her shoulder, "Don't you know that I need to rest up? School starts in three days!" Her bedroom door slammed.

"Thank God," Jamie muttered as the Rap music began blasting from behind the door. Maybe Kate, as a schoolteacher, knew some nifty tricks for handling teenagers. It would be nice to have someone to discuss the more complicated issues and tell him what he was doing wrong.

Then Jamie caught himself. Here he was, thinking as if Kate and he were already a team, and there *she* was, still hemming and hawing over Love Bytes.

As Millie would say, *Haw! Haw! Haw! The joke's on Huck!*

He stared at the blinking cursor awaiting his command. And whom would the joke be on if he went through with Stage Three, otherwise known as *Anything Goes*, of his anti-Love Bytes campaign and actually manipulated his score? Kate, just for thinking she could control the admittedly scary odds of having a successful marriage?

Or himself, for thinking that fudging his own sorry Love Bytes ranking could win him Kate's respect?

Would he even want to marry a woman who'd say yes only if her computer told her to?

Probably. He'd take her any way he could get her.

But maybe not. He deserved better.

Kate did, too.

Jamie shut off the computer.

LOVE BYTES WAS MAKING its final run and Kate was miserable. She pressed the button to set the printer and then raced at almost breakneck speed out of her office. She couldn't just sit back and watch.

Instead she went into the kitchen and made a cup of tea. The sound of the printer seemed to echo through the entire house. Hurriedly Kate snatched up a saucer and took her teacup into the backyard garden.

Butterflies danced among the crazy quilt patches of yellow and orange and green and purple. One of them flitted to a tuft of pale blue larkspur. "*Vanessa polychloros, Delphinium virescens,*" Kate recited to soothe her mind, then gave up the effort. Not even Latin could comfort her now.

Which meant she must have it really, really bad.

The big weeping willow swayed invitingly in the breeze, and Kate went to sit beneath the tree, sheltered by the privacy of the branches that drooped almost to the ground.

The day was warm with summer sunshine, but autumn wasn't far off. "Change is in the air," was what people said about this time of year.

For her, for once, big change.

Sitting in the grass, trying to clear her mind, Kate came to see how crucial it was that she make a decision *before* looking at the name of Love Bytes' choice for her perfect husband. It was only fair, for Jamie's sake, and just as much for her own.

The decision was surprisingly easy.

No way could she marry someone else, and if Love Bytes should select Jamie, she certainly didn't want to go to him spouting statistics instead of words of love and commitment.

Ah, there was the rub!

She wasn't good at taking risks, and that was what marriage was—the biggest risk of all. Yet people got married every day without agonizing overmuch about it. On the other hand, they got divorced, too, *with* a lot of agony.

Her timidity in this arena was why, before Jamie, she'd been able to go on 1,164 dates without baring her heart. The possibility of making a mistake that would cause her major upheaval and wrenching heartache scared her as much as the huge emotions of being in love used to.

Used to? The past tense had been automatic. She mulled that over. She *used to* be afraid of falling in love . . . but was no longer?

Not exactly, she decided. She was still scared, but being with Jamie had made her realize that to find true love you had to risk it being only infatuation. And that the reward was worth the risk.

Then it automatically followed that taking the final risk had to be worth it, too.

Kate's sudden laughter sparkled with joy. The entire conundrum was, after all of her endless fretting, only a matter of simple logic.

And magic, she silently added as she rose to her feet, parted the leafy green curtain of the willow and stepped out into the sunshine. *Very unscientific magic.*

She walked straight inside and up to her office, each footstep measured and sure. Nothing Love Bytes had to say could change her mind, but it would be sort of nice to know that her theories had not been entirely cockeyed.

The printer was quiet and the computer had switched to its swimming rainbow trout screensaver. Kate approached the stack of paper in the printer tray and selected only the top sheet. She could analyze the statistics later if she still cared to, but right now all she was interested in was the final result.

She closed her eyes, drew a deep breath, opened her eyes and turned the paper over fast before her brain could think of anything else to torture her with.

And there, in black and white, was the name of her perfect husband.

Jamie Flynn.

Kate's fist stabbed upward in an enthusiastic victory salute. Way to go, Love Bytes!

IT WAS EARLY EVENING, Huckleberries was half-filled and Jamie was carrying an armful of napkin packages and swizzle sticks, but still he spotted Kate the instant she stepped past the timbers of the open foyer. Even as she said hello to the waitress, Carole, and waved to someone else, her eyes were searching only for him. He was sure of it, and that plus the almost indiscernible but telling change in Kate's expression when she found him made something, some last little reserve of self-protection, give way inside.

Jamie flipped up the pass-through, ducked behind the bar and shoved the packages onto an already crowded shelf, then popped back up again. Without removing his gaze from the approaching Kate, he told Cecil, "Give the lady your seat," even though there were several unoccupied stools.

"My pleasure." Cecil stepped down, bobbing his head at Kate. "Your throne, m'dear," he said, making a sweeping gesture at the vacated place before going off to stake his claim on a booth.

Kate slid onto the stool. "Hey, bartender, give me a glass of your finest Bordeaux."

Jamie grinned. "Not a strawberry margarita?"

"Nope. I have a taste for a tart, full-bodied red. An irresistible craving, one might say."

"I can satisfy it."

His voice was like a caress. "That's what I hoped," Kate whispered as he set the glass of red wine on the bar before her. She dropped the crumpled sheet of paper she'd been reading and rereading all afternoon and lifted the glass to her lips. Her throat was dry and tight; the wine might help the former but only speaking her heart would cure the latter.

"What's that?" Jamie asked, indicating the paper.

She smoothed it out. "That's a long story."

"Give me the short version."

Nervousness flip-flopped through her, churning her up inside. Take the plunge, Kate, she told herself. *Take the risk.*

"Do you remember, a couple of nights ago, when I told you about catching the bouquet at another wedding?" Jamie nodded. "What I didn't say was that it was the fourth one I'd caught that year. And there's been three since, including Millie's even though Boris ripped it apart, which makes—"

"Seven," Jamie said, startled. "Jeez, Kate, you oughta warn a guy before you date him that you're a bride just waiting to happen."

"Although I didn't realize it at first, I've been waiting for a long time," she admitted. "Too long, in fact, so several months ago I decided to do something about it. I . . . I designed a computer program that would—" her words were running together faster and faster "—evaluate the men I'd dated all this year and choose which one was likely to be my best chance for a long-term commitment. In other words, the computer would pick out my future—"

"Husband."

Kate nodded. She'd crushed the last page of the printout in one fist, and when she realized what she'd done she carefully smoothed it out again, keeping it folded so the printing was facedown. "The computer program was called Love Bytes," she said, spelling the word.

"Clever," said Jamie. "But an oxymoron."

"I wasn't thinking clearly."

"And now you are?"

"I am." Kate looked up at Jamie speculatively. He wasn't expressing surprise, or curiosity. It was almost as if—

"You already knew!" she blurted out in amazement. "Somehow . . . *you knew.*"

Jamie leaned in closer, both elbows on the bar, so their exchange would be a bit more private. "Do you remember when I told you that Suze was being punished for hacking? She got Gregory Gordon Hodge to—"

"Oh, no!" Kate said, shocked to the marrow. "No. No. No. Please tell me they didn't see Love Bytes."

"They did, but they didn't know what it was," Jamie assured her. "I interrupted them before they had a chance to examine the printout."

"There's a printout?" The possibility appalled her.

"It was all a mistake. They were looking for Suze's summer school grade."

"But—" Kate's thoughts flew, adding up all the times she'd been suspicious of Jamie's choice of words, how they'd seemed to dovetail with Love Bytes. "Then only you knew?" she asked warily, wincing even at that. "For how long?"

"Oh, a while now, I guess."

He'd seen his own file! He'd seen his rank!

"I have to go," she said, pushing away from the bar. Blood roared in her ears; her face was on fire. Just today she'd realized how misguided Love Bytes was, but now the point had been driven home like a freight train. She could only imagine how Jamie must have felt about seeing himself graded in such a narrow, judgmental way.

"Don't go," he said, catching her arm.

"But you must hate me. With good reason."

"Do I look like I hate you?"

Kate slumped dejectedly. "No," she whispered. "But why not?"

"Because I understand why you did it." He touched her cold hands, rubbing his thumbs across the knobs of her knuckles, whitened from gripping the brass rail. "You told me so the other night."

Carole came up to the bar with an empty tray. "Sorry to interrupt, boss." She waved her order pad. "Bourbon water, two house reds, coffee black, Old Fashioned, Rolling Rock and, last but not least, Tom Folger wants a Zima. Hiya, Kate. How you doin'?"

Kate's gaze followed Jamie as he started setting up the drink order. "I couldn't say."

"You look nice."

"Thanks." She'd put on her best dress because it seemed the thing to wear for a proposal. Dressing for a funeral would have been more appropriate. She sneaked another look at Jamie. Maybe, maybe not.

He looked the same as usual, boy-next-door cute and open and sexy in loose-fit jeans and a cotton shirt with a wide red-and-white stripe. Her heart lightened. She might yet salvage the situation if Jamie truly understood that Love Bytes—no, *she*— hadn't meant to hurt him.

Carole loaded her tray off the pour pad and disappeared. Jamie got another beer and a bowl of peanuts for Roger, who looked out of place without Rex by his side. Kate's heart rate was approaching normal levels. Soon she'd even remember how to breathe.

"So," Jamie said.

She blinked.

"The paper?" he prompted.

Kate forced herself to push the final page of Love Bytes across the bar toward Jamie.

He picked it up, flipped it open and read his name. "Oh, I see," he said flatly. His lip lifted in a sneer.

Horrified, Kate realized that Jamie couldn't have cared less that he was Love Bytes' selection as her ideal mate. Her last hopes submerged in an ocean of abject misery.

Although Jamie had felt a momentary rush of pride at seeing his name on the paper, knowing it was the only reason Kate had come to claim him blunted the victory. Wanting him because a zillion numbers on a computer printout said she should wasn't good enough.

Deliberately he crushed the paper into a ball and tossed it over his shoulder. "So Love Bytes picked me and I'm supposed to be flattered," he said, his voice as raspy as sandpaper. "You've come here because your computer has decided that I'm good enough for you after all."

"No, Jamie," Kate pleaded, rising halfway off the bar stool, every inch of her straining toward him. "I know it looks like that—"

"It sure does. And there was a time that might have been enough for me. But now I want more." He gripped her by the forearms, lifting her another inch, drawing her face close to his. The Huckleberries patrons shushed each other and watched in near silence. Jamie and Kate were beyond noticing.

"I deserve more," Jamie said fiercely.

Kate's face went white. Her chin trembled. "You have it," she whispered. "I want to give you everything—love, commitment, laughter, babies..." She paused to lick her parched lips. "*Respect*," she said, her voice hoarse.

"Because of Love Bytes?" he asked through a rising tide of exhilaration. He hardly needed to. The truth was swimming in Kate's liquid emerald eyes.

"I decided on you before I looked at that stupid piece of paper." She blinked rapidly. "You have to believe me, Jamie. Please, please believe me."

There was no question of that. Kate might have kept her scheme with the computer a secret, but he had no doubt that she was telling him the truth now. He wanted to shout in triumph. *Kate* had chosen him, not just Love Bytes!

Briefly he wondered if he should confess how he'd manipulated Gordon Hodge and Cotter Coleman, then decided that it wasn't an urgent matter. Maybe he'd tell her a few years from now, right after they'd celebrated their *fifth* anniversary with an evening of fantastic if-the-world-ends-now-I'm-dying-happy sex. Yeah, that was exactly when he'd tell her.

Kate was watching him, a wordless offer of love shimmering from her like a magical aura.

The sight made Jamie's upper lip curve, the corners tilting jauntily, his cheeks broadening as he smiled. And smiled. And smiled.

Tentatively Kate smiled back.

"I do," he said. "I do believe you."

She slithered back onto the stool, her bones going as liquid as huckleberry jam. "You'd better watch what you're saying, Jamie. I thought I heard an 'I do.'"

Their friends and customers gasped as Jamie suddenly vaulted over the mahogany bar with one smooth, gymnastic maneuver. He bounced off the balls of his feet and efficiently spun Kate's stool around. She'd flung her hands up in surprise, but now her arms encircled Jamie's neck as he lifted her, his hands at her rib cage holding her high against his chest.

Kate was pink and giggly as she slid lower to find his mouth with hers. The witnesses had begun to applaud. Among the exclamations and cheering could be heard a raucous "Way to go, Huck! Haw! Haw! Haw!"

"I'm going to marry you," Jamie said into Kate's ear.

"*Yes*," she agreed.

"I'm going to give you beautiful redheaded babies," he whispered, adding wryly, "Not including Suze."

Kate's fingers sank into his thick auburn hair. "We could get started right away," she whispered back. "I've been considering a computer program that would do for baby making what Love Bytes did for—"

Jamie stopped her. "Katy, darling, pardon me for saying so, but you're a blockhead."

"What?" she squeaked.

"It's time you learned, teach," he said. "There are just some things that have to be done the old-fashioned way."

And then his mouth glided into place against hers, his lips as agile and irreverent as hers were first prim, then soft and sweet with loving. In other words, they were a perfect fit.

Epilogue

THE WEDDING TOOK PLACE at a small church in Belle Terre, but the reception was held outdoors at Whistler and Charity Castle's homestead.

Luckily, it was a fine autumn day, clear, crisp and glorious with color, the leaves painted in deep reds, flaming oranges, sovereign gold. Benches, chairs and long tables loaded with a celebratory feast had been set up in the pasture that Whistler and Charity had deeded over to Kate and Jamie as a wedding present. Jamie could be seen pointing out the perfect spot for their new house—beside the huckleberry patch where Kate had first swooned over him.

The wedding cake was not particularly expensive or elaborate, but it was iced between layers with sweet huckleberry jam. Placed on top, instead of the traditional bride and groom, was a tiny marzipan replica of a computer. The wedding guests didn't get the reference, and Kate and Jamie refused to explain. With the exception of Monica Danielson, Gregory Gordon Hodge was the only one who suspected the truth, and he was too busy chasing Suzannah up to the hayloft in the barn to care.

The groom was dashing in a black tuxedo with stylish accents of black velvet. The bride was elegant in a sophisticated dress with a champagne-colored velvet bodice and a full, moire-satin skirt of the same shade. She carried a very special bouquet that she was looking forward to throwing away.

That moment came when the cake was crumbs, the sun had dipped low and gusting winds were rippling through the fields of autumn gold. With Jamie by her side and all the unmarried ladies gathered before her, Kate gave her bridal bouquet one last, fond look. Nestled among the autumn dahlias, champagne roses and grape ivy were seven dried flowers; the unscientific but very romantic part of Kate had carefully preserved them from each of the bouquets she'd caught that year.

Kate kissed Jamie, winked at the eager Yvette and prepared to toss the bouquet to the next lucky bride.

As she cocked her arm, a strong breeze carried through the pasture, sending brittle leaves swirling all around the wedding party like a bright shower of confetti. Kate heaved back her arm and threw the bouquet.

A gust of wind caught it and tossed it right back at her. Having had so much practice, she caught the bouquet instinctively, laughing with surprise and delight over the unexpected but so appropriate gift.

"You know what this means, don't you?" she told Jamie, flinging her arms around his shoulders, the bouquet clenched tight in her fist where it belonged. "You're going to have to marry me again and again—every anniversary should do it."

His hazel eyes danced with mischief and merriment. "You want me to put up with all this wedding fuss and bother every autumn?" he asked, sounding doubtful. "You want me to put on this stuffed-shirt monkey suit once a year?"

"We'd also be forced to take a honeymoon," Kate observed. "At *least* once a year."

Jamie pretended to weigh the pros and cons. "Okay," he said at last, his grin at its most puckish, "you convinced me."

HARLEQUIN®
Temptation®

COMING NEXT MONTH

#601 THE HIGHWAYMAN Madeline Harper
Rogues, Book 5

When a quiet drive in the New York countryside turned into a time-travel trip from hell, Olivia Johnson *knew* her life would never be the same. Not only did she find herself in 1796 England, but worse, she'd fallen madly in love with a notorious highwayman—a highwayman who would hang before the year was out....

#602 FOR THE THRILL OF IT Patricia Ryan

Thrill seeker and confirmed bachelor Clay Granger was tired of dodging matrimony. When his best friend, Izzy, revealed she was pregnant and deserted by another man, he saw a solution to *both* their problems. It might even be an adventure! But a platonic marriage wasn't easy when neither one really wanted it that way....

#603 MIDNIGHT TRAIN FROM GEORGIA Glenda Sanders
The Wrong Bed

Erica O'Leary wasn't expecting her trip to Baltimore to be a picnic. But when a rowdy group of Irish-American attorneys decided to continue their St. Patrick's Day partying on the train, it couldn't get any worse. At least she had a sleeping car! But when Erica woke up beside a gorgeous stranger, she knew her nightmare—or fantasy—had just begun!

#604 THE TEXAN TAKES A WIFE Kristine Rolofson
Mail Order Men

Ben Bradley wasn't thrilled when his matchmaking mother placed a personal ad in *Texas Men* magazine—*for him.* And when women started showing up at the ranch in droves, he'd had it! Little wonder he sought refuge with his sympathetic yet surprisingly sexy housekeeper....

Women throughout time have
lost their hearts to:

Starting in January 1996, Harlequin Temptation
will introduce you to five irresistible, sexy rogues.
Rogues who have carved out their place in history,
but whose true destinies lie in the arms of
contemporary women.

#569 *The Cowboy,* Kristine Rolofson
(January 1996)

#577 *The Pirate,* Kate Hoffmann
(March 1996)

#585 *The Outlaw,* JoAnn Ross
(May 1996)

#593 *The Knight,* Sandy Steen
(July 1996)

#601 *The Highwayman,* Madeline Harper
(September 1996)

Dangerous to love, impossible to resist!

Free Gift Offer

With a Free Gift proof-of-purchase
from any Harlequin® book, you can receive
a beautiful cubic zirconia pendant.

This stunning marquise-shaped stone is a genuine cubic
zirconia—accented by an 18" gold tone necklace.
(Approximate retail value $19.95)

Send for yours today...
compliments of &HARLEQUIN®

To receive your free gift, a cubic zirconia pendant, send us one original proof-of-purchase, photocopies not accepted, from the back of any Harlequin Romance®, Harlequin Presents®, Harlequin Temptation®, Harlequin Superromance®, Harlequin Intrigue®, Harlequin American Romance®, or Harlequin Historicals® title available in August, September or October at your favorite retail outlet, together with the Free Gift Certificate, plus a check or money order for $1.65 U.S./$2.15 CAN. (do not send cash) to cover postage and handling, payable to Harlequin Free Gift Offer. We will send you the specified gift. Allow 6 to 8 weeks for delivery. Offer good until October 31, 1996 or while quantities last. Offer valid in the U.S. and Canada only.

Free Gift Certificate

Name: _____

Address: _____

City: _____ State/Province: _____ Zip/Postal Code: _____

Mail this certificate, one proof-of-purchase and a check or money order for postage and handling to: HARLEQUIN FREE GIFT OFFER 1996. In the U.S.: 3010 Walden Avenue, P.O. Box 9071, Buffalo NY 14269-9057. In Canada: P.O. Box 604, Fort Erie, Ontario L2Z 5X3.

Weddings by DeWilde

Since the turn of the century the elegant and fashionable DeWilde stores have helped brides around the world turn the fantasy of their "Special Day" into reality. But now the store and three generations of family are torn apart by the separation of Grace and Jeffrey DeWilde. Family members face new challenges and loves in this fast-paced, glamorous, internationally set series. For weddings and romance, glamour and fun-filled entertainment, enter the world of DeWildes...

Watch for TO LOVE A THIEF
by Margaret St. George
Coming to you in September 1996

DeWildes Monte Carlo was the site of a heist too good to be true. Security expert Allison Ames and cat burglar Paul Courtwald both wanted the Empress Catherine tiara, a piece of the famed DeWilde collection. Allies for the wrong reasons, they found themselves lovers... for all the reasons that matter.

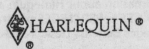

HARLEQUIN ®

®

Look us up on-line at: http://www.romance.net

WBD6

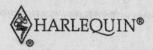